"Are you warmer yet?" David asked, pulling her closer.

Holding herself rigid in his arms, Allison said, "David, I—"

"Ssh," he ordered, pausing on the threshold of the kiss, savoring the anticipation. You could only kiss a woman for the first time once, and he wanted to fulfill the potential that lay in her soft, shell-pink lips.

"You—you'll catch my cold," she whispered, her body switching on like a furnace. A wash of heat swept from her toes to her hair, and she swayed slightly in his embrace.

"I'll take my chances," he said huskily, and bending down, pressed his mouth to hers.

His kiss was gentle, reassuring, almost courtly as his satiny lips brushed hers. "Detective Jones," he murmured, nuzzling her temple. "Your hair smells like a spring rain, oh lovely Allison." He kissed her again, and her eyes shut tightly as a startled excitement rose over her. Everywhere at once her body burst into flames— but he gave her nothing to burn with his tender, undemanding kiss. Instead, the heat built inside her, smoking out everything but the utter delight of him, this stranger who had sought her out like a sleuth on a case, Bogie searching for Ingrid, Jimmy Stewart hunting for Grace Kelly . . .

WHAT ARE *LOVESWEPT* ROMANCES?

They are stories of true romance and touching emotion. We believe those two very important ingredients are constants in our highly sensual and very believable stories in the *LOVESWEPT* line. Our goal is to give you, the reader, stories of consistently high quality that may sometimes make you laugh, sometimes make you cry, but are always fresh and creative and contain many delightful surprises within their pages.

Most romance fans read an enormous number of books. Those they truly love, they keep. Others may be traded with friends and soon forgotten. We hope that each *LOVESWEPT* romance will be a treasure—a "keeper." We will always try to publish

LOVE STORIES YOU'LL NEVER FORGET
BY AUTHORS YOU'LL ALWAYS REMEMBER

The Editors

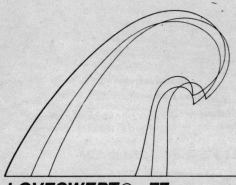

LOVESWEPT® · 77

Nancy Holder
Finders Keepers

BANTAM BOOKS
TORONTO · NEW YORK · LONDON · SYDNEY · AUCKLAND

FINDERS KEEPERS

A Bantam Book / January 1985

*LOVESWEPT® and the wave device are registered trademarks
of Bantam Books, Inc. Registered in U.S. Patent and Trademark
Office and elsewhere.*

ISBN 0-553-21684-4

Published simultaneously in the United States and Canada

*Bantam Books are published by Bantam Books, Inc. Its
trademark, consisting of the words ''Bantam Books'' and the
portrayal of a rooster, is Registered in U.S. Patent and Trademark Office and in other countries. Marca Registrada. Bantam
Books, Inc., 666 Fifth Avenue, New York, New York 10103.*

PRINTED IN THE UNITED STATES OF AMERICA

O   0 9 8 7 6 5 4 3 2 1

To Elise, Sandra, Richard Jr., & David Wilkinson,
and Pat Adams-Manson:

peace and love.

And to the confirmed bachelors of the world:

Here's looking at you, kids.

One

"Thanks, Mr. King," crooned the woman as David held the door open for her. He towered over her, his height giving him a great view of her spangled bikini top and all that nestled within it. Though she'd wrapped a coat around herself, she'd let it slip open on her journey from the head of the table to the door.

Smiling, he saluted her, touching his hand to his wavy black hair. His chestnut eyes grew hooded as she brushed his forearm, her fingers pale against his tanned skin.

"You did a great job," David told her, pressing a fifty-dollar bill into her hand

She winked at him, wrapping the money around her finger. "Hey, I'll take my clothes off for you anytime." She raked him with her eyes, apparently liking what she saw. "You're not married, are you?"

He laughed. "No, but I'm the only one who isn't."

"One's all I need," she replied saucily, and swaggered out of the back room of Club Hubba Hubba.

Behind him, the hooting and applauding had begun to subside. David turned around and looked at his friends, surveying the scene with satisfaction. Everyone he'd invited had come. Two dozen men had been rollicking here for four hours—guzzling liquor, guffawing at raunchy jokes, ogling Delita, the exotic dancer who'd

2 • NANCY HOLDER

just left, and generally needling Bob Campbell about his upcoming ordeal. In short, they were having a marvelous time.

"How come the ladies always go for you, King?" Bernie, a friend from the old cabbie days, frowned at David and scratched his balding head. "Geez, this guy has to beat them off with a stick! What's he got that we don't?" he asked the others.

"Hair, Bernie," somebody threw back.

"Women think tall men have it where it counts," another man offered. "If they only knew poor David's a midget in that department—"

"Damn, if that's what you think, you've never gone to the gym with him," Bernie muttered. "The King's got a scepter that's eleven inches—"

"Bring back Velveeta!" someone cried out drunkenly.

"You guys're degenerating," said Bob, the guest of honor. He gestured toward the empty chair on his left and frowned. "Siddown, David," he mumbled, raising another drink to his lips. "I haven't talked t'you all evening."

"Sure thing, Bob," David replied, grinning the crooked grin that had endeared him to the thousands of women who'd read page thirty-five of *San Francisco's Most Watchable Bachelors—Could They be Waiting for YOU?* "I've always got time to comfort the condemned."

He folded his tremendous height into the wooden captain's chair and poured himself a glass of Scotch. It was a cut above the usual stuff served at the Hubba. Bubba, the owner, had imported it for the occasion.

And what an occasion it was, he thought wistfully. Bob was the last to go; the last of his bachelor buddies to be getting married. At thirty-two, David was the only one left.

"Here's t' marriage!" Bob bellowed, trying to rise from his chair. But he fell back with a grunt, blinked, and tapped glasses with David. Then he swallowed his drink in two long gulps and gasped as he slammed the glass on the table.

His head wobbled as he looked up at David. "I'm getting married," he said wonderingly. "David, you should get married too."

David laughed. "Not on your life."

"We all go, sooner or later," Bernie said. "Look at Bob."

"Look at all of us," Stu added ruefully, slogging down more beer.

"Not me. No way." David leaned back in his chair and crossed his hands behind his head. "I'm the exception to that rule, old friends."

"There are no exceptions," someone said soberly. "It's a law of nature."

"It's not in my nature," David insisted.

Bob guffawed. "Are you willin' to put your mouth where your money is?" He raised his hand. "I've got a hunnerd bucks says a year from t'night ol' David's hitched!"

Sam Debussy stood up. "And I say he's a free man!" He saluted David with a tumbler full of tequila. "Long live the eternal bachelor! May he sow his wild oats forever!"

David grinned. "I'll drink to that."

Voices rose in a babble as men joined in the wager. Bottles toppled over. Ashtrays sailed to the floor. The boys snickered and chortled and Bob punched David's arm a little harder than usual.

"You'd better not let me down," Stu said to David, stuffing his mouth with beer nuts and pretzels. "This time next year, you'd better be a free man!"

David laughed. "Not to worry," he drawled, savoring his drink. "That's one bet you'll never lose."

"Men!" Allison Jones muttered. "This is it! No more! I'm giving them up for Lent!"

It occurred to her, as she listened to the click-click-click of her low-heeled boots, that Lent was long past. And she, for that matter, wasn't of a religious persuasion that observed Lenten sacrifices.

"For the Fourth of July, then," she said as she continued walking down the littered street.

The summer fog had crept up from San Francisco Bay, inching toward the private-eye moon that hung above the notorious North Beach district of the city. The fog gauzed the light from the lampposts, casting a misty aura around Allison, accenting with gleaming midnight blue the raven curls that caressed her earlobes. Her eyes shone in the light, crystal sapphires, huge as a doe's, sharp as a cat's. Her boots echoed on the pavement as she strolled on.

Allison paused beneath one of the lamps, scrutinizing first her map and then the street. Pawnshops clustered next to bars and mission outreaches in the swirling gray. Sailors and bag ladies trundled past, heads turning at the sight of the diminutive woman in trench coat and fedora who stared back at them with a practiced and most indifferent air.

With a casualness that belied her uneasy pique, she moved on down the street. North Beach was not her scene—not at all, with its leather-jacketed, scowling teenagers and its winos leaning against windows ablaze with beer signs and invitations to SEE THE GIRLS! GIRLS! GIRLS! But she boldly went forth where no member of the San Francisco Jones clan had gone before, wherever the cases and clients took her. And tonight she had serious business on the seamier side of Columbus Avenue.

Nevertheless, she took her time. She always did. There were a million details to notice on a street like this and she wasn't about to let one slip by. A million stories in the half-naked city; a million cases to crack. In her profession, being observant was very important. So was keeping her cool when all around her were losing theirs. She liked to think she did a laudable job of both. Her track record attested to the effectiveness of her methods, at any rate—she almost always got her creature.

It was nearly eleven o'clock when she reached her destination. She chuckled at the name painted on the double doors: Club Hubba Hubba. Noting the peeling paint and broken neon sign, she figured there wasn't too much in there that belonged in a class with the bee's knees or the cat's meow. But a man was waiting inside for her, and from the sound of his voice on the phone earlier that evening, he was a desperate man indeed.

She hesitated a moment, aware that she was a small, lone woman entering what was obviously a male retreat. Relax, Allison, she told herself. Miss Marple would think nothing of ambling into a place like this. Even Nancy Drew would go for it. It came with the territory; it was part of the job. Humphrey Bogart would take it in stride. And, to the eternal mystification of her entire family, this was the only job she wanted.

"So, here's looking at you, kid," she said resolutely, and pushed the doors open.

In the back room they'd begun to tease David unmercifully.

"Don'cha wanna little woman?" Bernie asked. "Don'cha wanna kid who needs braces and wears safety pins in his ears?"

David smiled smugly.

"Huh, you jus' wait," Bob said thickly. "You'll see. It happens to all of us." He smiled. "You got my wedding ring wi' you?"

"Yes." David cocked his head and drew the small velvet case out of his pocket. "But you told me to keep it till the ceremony."

"I jus' wanna see it," Bob said, opening the box. He let out a sly chuckle and held the diamond-encrusted band to the light. Then, without warning, he picked up David's hand and shoved the ring on his wedding finger.

"Hey!" David cried. He felt a flash of pain as the groom-to-be forced the ring past the second knuckle, catching the short, curly hairs on his finger.

"Get used to it," Bob murmured, his head lolling against the back of his chair. "I'll buy yours for you wi' all the money I'm gonna make off this bet."

"Don't hold your breath, Campbell," David said, tugging at the ring. "Damn! This thing is stuck!"

"Get used to it." Bob chuckled. His eyes closed and his body bowed forward.

"Better not," Stu cut in. "We're counting on you, King."

David looked down at the ring as if it were a diseased growth infecting his finger. "There's never been a surer thing, guys. Believe me. There's no way I'm getting married this year."

Allison had miraculously made her way across the crowded room to the bar and introduced herself to the most desperate-looking man there. Now, seated on one of the vinyl-covered stools, she unbuttoned the top of her trench coat as the heat and noise enveloped her.

The place was a dive, as she had expected. Everything was veiled in a haze of smoke, wrapped in a pulsating curtain of disco music that throbbed from a dozen speakers. Beyond a quartet of pool tables, a woman dressed in a fire-engine red miniskirt and chemise shimmied on a tiny platform.

Allison sighed, then assumed an expression of authority and competence as she continued her dossier on Subject No. 457—The Case of the Scampering Shar-Pei.

"Please, Raphael," she said to her client, "try not to cry. I need the facts if I'm going to find Bruce Lee for you."

Raphael, the bartender, was a slight, pale man with buffed nails, a diamond in his ear, and a lisp he obviously thought quite fetching. At the moment he was weeping openly, unable to finish mixing the batch of drinks the cocktail waitress had requested. Dressed in a brief Roman toga, the waitress stood with her arms akimbo, chomping on a wad of spearmint gum that made Allison's eyes water.

Allison crossed her arms over her chest and reached with the heels of her boots for the brass rail below the stool. She was so short that there was no real hope of finding it, of course, but she had never been one to give up a search.

The gentle bartender let out a huge sob.

"Raphael," she said kindly.

He wiped his eyes with a pastel pink handkerchief. "I know, I know," he murmured. "I'm sorry, Detective Jones. But it was getting so late and I was so worried you wouldn't come!"

"I was . . . detained," she said, frowning as she remembered the fiasco at her apartment earlier that evening.

Why, after six months, had Ed Martin taken it into his head to "pop by" tonight to pick up his Rod McKuen records? And why had Ironside, her three-legged Siamese, taken it into *her* head to have kittens on top of those very records three days earlier?

And how could Barry have picked tonight to go for the Christian Science church near the park? Even now her demented nephew was down at the police station waiting for her to bail him out on trespassing charges. The desk sergeant had called while she was trying to apologize to Ed for the loss to the world of poetry.

"The human fly and the man with no taste," she muttered disgustedly. Why had they conspired to make her so late for her appointment? Because they're men, she decided, excusing Ironside on the grounds of motherhood. And boy, she thought, do I sound like a bitter old spinster tonight! Well, after all, I'm almost twenty-nine.

"I'm sorry about being late," she said. "Believe me, Raphael, it won't happen again."

"I'm just so distraught!" Raphael went on, adding a twist of lime to a margarita and handing it to the waitress. "I'm in such agony!"

"I know," Allison said soothingly. "I understand."

Her response wasn't phony; she did know what it was like to lose a pet. She knew it was a jungle out there on the streets of San Francisco. Not a day went by that a desperate bulldog or a remorseful German shepherd didn't wander through the fog, grieving for the home and hearth he had so recklessly abandoned—in a snit, perhaps, or to chase after some foolish dream: a cat, a pigeon, a fire engine.

Allison patted Raphael's arm. She knew. She understood. She carried a license; she searched the byways and alleys for lost canines and felines. She was a pet detective!

Raphael put the handkerchief back in his pocket and touched his fingers to the corners of his eyes. "If I'm not careful, I'm going to wrinkle," he said, sniffling. "Oh, this is wearing me down!"

"Are you too worn down to get me some more whiskey and tequila?" a deep masculine voice intruded. Both Allison and Raphael turned in its direction, and Allison nearly fell off her stool when its owner brushed by her and laid a clutch of empties on the bar.

Oh, she thought, nearly voicing the word. Oh, oh, oh.

To begin with, he was very tall, way over six feet. He stood erect as he divested himself of the bottles, not stooping the way some unusually tall men did. Up in the stratosphere, his hair was as black as her own, though not nearly as curly. It had a nice wavy texture and it was well cut, accentuating his sharp sculpted cheekbones and jaw, aquiline nose, and high sweeping forehead. His lashes, which Allison would have killed for, framed chestnut eyes that glittered in the harsh lights above the bar.

"Sure thing," Raphael replied, his cheeks pink. He practically fluttered his lids at the stranger as he cleared the bar of the empty bottles. "Bubba told me to take real good care of you."

"Thanks," the man said amiably. Full lips parted as he whistled silently to himself, jingling the change in his pocket.

Allison swallowed. A real TDH, as Janet would say. Tall, dark and handsome. The incredible hunk.

He must have felt her staring, for he turned toward

her and flashed a quick smile. Then he did a classic double take, his eyes widening, his lips parting in surprise.

"Well, hello," he said, grinning. It was a crooked sort of grin, boyish and appraising all at once, and Allison felt the bones in her back and shoulders begin to dissolve. His gaze swept up and down her body as he took a step closer. Her muscles started to melt as well.

The grin turned into a bright, flashing smile. For a moment Allison thought he assumed he knew her. His expression was warm and confident, as if he were greeting an old friend.

Friend? Come on, Allison, she chided herself. This guy is reducing you to a puddle on the floor. On purpose. He's checking you out.

And evidently deciding it would be nice to check in. He slid onto the bar stool beside hers and laid his right hand on the varnished wood near her notebook. Her fingers tingled and she picked up her pencil. Lauren Bacall would have a cigarette, she thought vaguely. Unlighted, so he could do it for her. And then she'd lean that marvelous head back and blow smoke at those ridiculous cone-shaped lights up there . . .

Watch it, Allison, a small voice chided. You've given up on the male sex. And this man is definitely a sex—er, a member. She flushed. A member of the male—

"Taking notes?" the man asked.

"Of a sort." She shifted on her stool. He smells so good, she thought. Like pine trees and new-mown hay. And soap. He smells like a clean, sexy guy.

In a dirty, raunchy bar.

His abundant lashes drooped, hooding his lids in a decidedly come-hither way. "Learning anything?" he drawled, tracing the wet circles on the bar. His fingers were long, his nails neatly trimmed. On the little finger—which was actually fairly large—he wore a silver ring engraved with a monogram: DKR. Daniel? Dusty? Divine?

"Now, Raphael," she said, trying to clear her throat

without making any noise, "how old did you say Bruce Lee is?"

At the mention of his dog's name, the bartender's lower lip began to tremble. "He's in the terrible twos. He's been just impossible lately."

The other man's brows rose, but he said nothing, just tapped his fingers on the bar in time to the music. He was wearing a perfectly tailored blue shirt, the sleeves folded back to reveal forearms sprinkled with long, dark hair. A complicated-looking digital watch, expensive and shiny, caught the light as his wrist moved. He seemed coiled with energy that was barely contained inside him, as if he might burst apart with things to do and people to see.

Like whom? she wondered. What was a nice man like him doing in a place like this?

"You've just got to find him," Raphael pleaded. "He's my little China doll."

The stranger smiled to himself and continued to tap the bar. Raphael put down two more bottles of Scotch, grimaced at the hunk, and wrung his hands. "Listen, I've got to get the tequila out of the storage room," he fretted. "Would you mind waiting a minute? And if anybody comes—"

"I'll tell them to hang on," the man said soothingly. Raphael flashed him a radiant smile and trotted off.

The radiant smile reappeared on the man's face. "Alone at last," he quipped, giving her That Grin again.

"Hardly," she retorted, not meaning to sound so prim.

Her detective's eyes slid lower. Oh, she thought, noting the spot where man met bar stool. He must play a lot of tennis. Or racquetball. Maybe he jogs. Whatever he does, it's . . . effective.

"Looking for something?" he asked.

Her cheeks blazed as she looked up at him. There was a smug, sassy look on his face that told her he knew what she'd been looking at.

"Finding it?" he continued.

"I'm working," she replied, picking up her pencil and rolling it between her hands.

His eyes widened and he glanced at the dance platform, where the glory that was Rome was now dancing. Chomping her gum, she was in the process of unbuckling the medallion that held her toga together. He looked back at Allison with question marks, and she covered her chest with her arms. Never in her wildest dreams would she be Club Hubba Hubba dancer material, and she knew it. She suspected Mr. TDH must have noticed her lack of . . . qualifications as well.

"Not like that," she muttered. "I'm here to see Raphael."

"Mr. Pink Hankie?" he asked, the questioning look spreading from eyes to brows to lips. He had a scar just below his nose and she wondered vaguely how he'd gotten it. She wondered what his name was. And she wondered—barely allowing the thought into the conscious part of her mind—if he was, ah, well-proportioned all over.

Heavens, Allison, for somebody who's just given up men, you're certainly acting bizarrely, she chided herself. But she doubted even a saint could keep her thoughts on purer things when confronted with a handsome devil like this.

"What are you drinking?" he asked, glancing down at the territory near her notebook and hands. "Can I get you something? A glass of white wine? Some cognac?"

Some smelling salts? A cold shower? He started to slide off the stool, but Allison shook her head. "No, thanks," she said. He was much better dressed than the other men in the joint. He looked like a millionaire. Maybe he owned the place. Looking around at the peeling paint and the dusty light fixtures, she found the idea mildly depressing.

"All right." He sat back down, apparently content just to smile at her and wait for his tequila. It made her nervous, this breezy confidence of his, the way he lounged beside her as if he had a perfect right to chitchat while she went into a mild state of catatonia. Mesmerizing good looks, she thought wonderingly. He's got them. They really do exist. Wait till I tell Janet.

"Do you live near here?" the man asked, leaning his arm on the bar, almost touching her fingers. "I don't think I've seen you around before."

Lines. He was throwing out his hook, waiting to see how the fishing was. A part of her was flattered, but most of her went on alert.

"No," she said simply. "I've never been here before."

"But you're *working*?" It was a leading question, and the way he slid his glance toward her made her sit up straight—though her nose barely came to his chest— and throw back her shoulders.

"Yeah," she said blandly. "I'm picking up sailors."

His eyes crinkled, the corners of his lips twitched. Wonderful lips. Wonderful crinkles.

"I own a catamaran," he said.

She couldn't hold back a little smile. That grin of his was really charming. It almost made her forget to be nervous.

Almost. She shrugged, unable to think of a comeback worthy of his. She was a bit rusty in the flirtation department.

And rustier still in the singles' scene department . . .

"I'm working for Raphael, to find his dog," she confessed, feeling decidedly unglamorous as she said it. Ingrid Bergman would have been a mysterious foreign spy; Joan Crawford a sophisticated lady in distress— though too proud, of course, to admit it. But Allison Elizabeth Jones was a short, wary pet detective.

"Oh, you're a friend, then?" He wasn't going to give up easily. He continued to smile at that amazing smile, probably very aware that it was making her zing like an alternating current.

"No. We just met." She liked him, she thought, appalled. She was attracted to him and wanted him to try to pick her up. Oh, dear, she had to get out of here.

"I wonder where Raphael is," she muttered. "I've got another appointment soon."

"At midnight?"

She toyed with her pencil. "I work late sometimes."

He regarded her for a moment. "You mean, this really is your job?"

"My profession," she corrected him.

"You look for lost dogs?"

"Dogs, cats, turtles—anything."

"No kidding." He scratched his chin. "Can you make a living at it?"

"I get by."

"I could never accept just getting by," he said with sudden intensity. He became almost grave, his eyes fathomless as amber pools. "Never."

"So you'd say you're doing all right?" she asked, emboldened by his sudden introspection. If he could ask personal questions, so could she. After all, perhaps he'd realized Bruce Lee was a valuable animal and had kidnapped him. One could never be too sure in cases like these. Audrey Hepburn had once even suspected Cary Grant . . .

His reflective mood passed as quickly as it had come. "Yeah," he said. With his crooked grin in place, he looked almost cynical. "I'm doing all right."

"Good thing."

"I know a good thing when I see one," he murmured, looking straight at her.

She felt as if he'd touched her, as if those silky lashes were silky fingertips sliding down the sides of her face, tracing the curve of her jaw, trailing down her neck. As if his lips had pressed against her cheek, her temple, coming to rest at last on her mouth. In her mind's eye she saw him unbuttoning her trench coat, drawing away the oyster-colored shirt beneath, filling his hands with her breasts . . .

"Where's that Raphael?" she blurted out. What was wrong with her? She didn't usually have sexy fantasies about strange men. Well, maybe a few stray ones about

Laurence Olivier and Tyrone Power, but not about everyday strangers, not like this.

But this man was not everyday material. This man was incredible.

"Look," she said, shaken, "please tell Raphael—"

As she started to speak, a man came up and set down an empty glass. At once the hunk slid off his stool and walked around the bar.

"What'll it be?" he asked the man.

"Bourbon and water," came the reply.

The TDH measured out the bourbon with flair, then added the water and a swizzle stick. He took the man's money, and made change, and received a tip for his trouble, which he popped into a ceramic bank shaped like a hot dog.

Smiling at Allison, he wiped his hands on the dish towel and sat back down on his stool.

"All in a day's work," he said, answering her unspoken question. "Bubba gave me a job here when I first blew into town." And, oh, Lord, he thought, had he needed a job.

"Bubba?"

"He owns the Hubba."

He chuckled at the same time she did, his chest vibrating with the sound. She looked at it and saw dark hairs peeking out above an unbuttoned shirt collar. His chest was broad, his shoulders broader. Allison swallowed and picked up her purse.

"Listen," she said, "I really do have to go. I have to . . . pick up someone."

"What's wrong? Is his boat bigger than mine?"

Ignoring him, she dug into her wallet and produced one of her business cards. It showed a beagle wearing a Sherlock Holmes cap and cape, staring with one huge eye through a magnifying glass. ALLISON JONES, PET DETECTIVE read the old-fashioned script. Under it were her address and phone number.

"Please give this to Raphael," she said, thrusting it at him. "Tell him I'll be in all day tomorrow."

His brows rose with interest. Taking his left hand out of his pocket, he brushed her outstretched fingers as he collected the trophy of her phone number. "All day, you say?"

His touch was more thrilling than she had imagined. It was like stroking warm velvet, and it sent a jolt through her fingertips, past her wrist, and up her arm. It caused such a uniquely pleasant sensation that she glanced down at his hand, at the strength and size of his fingers . . .

Her lips formed an O of surprise and chagrin. "You're married," she said slowly.

Plucking the card from her, he examined the wedding ring and said, "Oh, this? It's nothing, really. Just a joke."

"A joke." She narrowed her eyes at him and gathered up her purse. Now she didn't need to ask what a nice man like him was doing here. Because he wasn't nice. He was flirting with her and he was a married man. He was a jerk.

"I see," she said, cheeks flaming. With as much dignity as she could muster, she gave her stool a half-turn and grabbed the bar with one hand, praying for a graceful, four point landing.

Alas, it was not to be. Faster than she could cry "Geronimo!" her boot heel caught on the rail she'd searched for before. She raised her foot, but only succeeded in bashing her instep. Meanwhile, her momentum pulled her off the seat and she fell forward, nearly toppling face-first onto the empty stool in front of her.

Huffing, she struggled to extricate herself. Too late—his big hands wrapped themselves around her forearms and did it for her.

"You don't understand," he said. "The ring's just a gag. I'm here with a bunch of friends and—"

She shrugged him off as her boots clattered onto the floor. Smoothing her trench coat, she turned around. "Look, it doesn't matter. After all, we're never going to see each other again."

He frowned slightly. "Never . . .?" He glanced down at her business card. "I was assuming that you gave—"

The door of the back room burst open and a gaggle of men staggered out.

"David! Let's party!" one bellowed.

At that moment a loud beeping pierced the air. Allison watched as the TDH—David—swore under his breath and pulled a beeper off his belt.

She was losing her touch, Allison thought vaguely. She hadn't even noticed that thing.

Glancing in her direction, he punched a button and said, "Go ahead."

As a metallic voice began to deliver its message, he held a hand out to her. But she was already burrowing her way across the room to the front doors.

"Wait a minute!" he called. "Listen! I'm not—"

"David, come on!" another man cried.

Allison gave a determined tug to her fedora, raised her chin, and with great dignity marched out of Club Hubba Hubba.

Once outside, she leaned against the wall, exhaling. Damn, she thought. He was so handsome too.

"Allison Jones, shame on you," she muttered aloud, pulling herself away from the building. "You know you've promised yourself to stay away from fires. And that one's a bonfire, blazing out of control."

She turned the corner, pausing to catch her breath again. An old derelict staggered across the street, his tattered coat flapping around his knees.

"All right, all right," she went on, "I didn't do anything, did I? I mean, I'm out here alone, aren't I?"

You'd darn well better be, a voice inside her head growled. A married man!

She walked past the derelict, bobbing her head. "Good evening, officer," she said.

The man's vacant stare melted away, leaving a little frown in its place.

"How'd you know I was a cop?" he asked plaintively.

"I have an eye for detail," she replied, walking on.

But not necessarily a keen one.

Inside the Hubba, David had declared an end to the party.

"It's time to get you home to bed," he told Bob, "so you can get some sleep before I have to sober you up."

"You're a prinsh," Bob said, standing on tiptoe as he tried to fling his arm around David's shoulder. "Hey, you grew!"

"We're going to have to get this ring off too," David said, tugging at the band. He closed his eyes and laughed silently as he remembered how Allison—he liked that name—had flounced off when she'd seen it.

Maybe we should leave it on, he thought absently. A look of horror came over his face as he herded his friend—the last bachelor friend he had—out the door.

Two

The next morning Allison called Raphael and completed her dossier on his Chinese fighting dog. Fittingly enough, he'd made his bolt for freedom in Chinatown. "I suppose he was homesick," Raphael told her, still sniffling.

The wind was up in Chinatown and the rain was about to come down, belying the early-morning promise of a sunny day. This was common in San Francisco in June, positively the worst month to entertain somebody from out of town.

And if anybody was from somewhere else, it was her nephew, Barry, a strapping boy of sixteen. He was the image of Allison's sister Maribeth, who had gotten both the good name and the height. And who was the family pet, having become a child psychologist, *and* married a surgeon, *and* given birth to Barry Jameson Osgood—the first and thus far only grandchild of Allison's parents.

And, unknown to said grandparents, possibly harboring a few bats in his belfry.

Bats that Maribeth was bent on ignoring. A few hours ago she'd called from Portugal, one of the stops on her European vacation, and when Allison had tried to tell her about the incident with the police, Maribeth had laughed it off.

"He's just acting out," she'd told Allison. "Just give him some space. And Allison, I can't thank you enough for providing him with a secure environment while Michael and I are on our vacation."

That's right, Allison thought, turning to Barry. They were sitting in Tung Fat's Oriental Cuisine, sipping oolong tea. Maribeth couldn't thank her enough.

"No more crawling up the side of the house," Allison said to Barry. "Use the stairs like normal people."

"But I like to climb," Barry protested, but clamped his mouth shut at her quelling glance. She'd already delivered a scathing lecture on his fascination with tall buildings and their ledges and crannies.

"Next time, no bail," she said.

There was a moment's silence. Then Barry sighed and said, "I'm tired, Aunt Al. And it's starting to rain. Can't we go home now?"

She didn't respond. She was watching Mr. Fat, who had politely taken the flyer that requested information about Bruce Lee and was now slipping it into a menu. Dog was a delicacy in China. Perhaps he was a little homesick too, Allison fretted.

"Let's go home," Barry wheedled.

"And miss your chance to sight-see?" she asked, pouring him another scalding cup of tea. "What would your mother say if I didn't show you the city?"

His disultory reply was drowned out by a huge commotion outside. Car horns blared, and people laughed and shouted. Somebody began to clash cymbals and a crowd started to gather. It was like a miniature Chinese New Year's celebration.

"What's going on?" she asked the waiter, but he just shrugged and joined the throng at the door.

"Barry, can you see anything?" she asked, trying to peer through the windows that fronted the street. But she was too short to penetrate the great wall of diners who had stood up to get a better look.

"Come on," she ordered, tossing a dollar on the table. She hurried outside, hanging onto her fedora, strug-

gling not to hit anybody with her briefcase filled with flyers, and not to get blinded by the spokes of an oncoming
umbrella. And then she saw what the ruckus was all
about.

"Oh, how sweet!" she cried, and the elderly Chinese
lady beside her bobbed her bamboo parasol in agreement.

"How awesome!" Barry echoed, pulling his jacket over
his head in a vain attempt to hide from the spurts of
rain.

The ruckus was a huge white limousine, a Lincoln
Continental so long that it looked as if an extra car body
had been wedged between its three sets of doors. Its
tinted windows were slathered with the age-old sayings:
"Just Married!" and "Tonight's the Night!" and these
were beginning to foam back into soap. Along the glossy
sides of the elegant vehicle, paper roses and streamers
drooped in the drizzle, dribbling soft-hued rainbows
over the white sidewall tires.

The limo was idling in the middle of the road, and all
around it car horns were blaring and people were either
cheering or shouting at the driver to get out of the way.

Allison tried to peek through the windows, angling for
a decent view as the crowd flowed and eddied around
her. Under her fedora she could feel her curls plastering
themselves to her forehead. The poor bride and groom!
What if they were stuck?

"Barry, can you see?" she called to him.

"Yeah, there's a guy behind the wheel," he said. "He's
dressed up."

Then the front door opened. A man climbed out with
easy elegance, a tall one, with hair as dark as Allison's,
though not so curly. His splendid, semi-familiar shoulders were molded by a dove-gray cutaway coat, and he
wore a white high-collared shirt with a gray and white
ascot, a vest of a darker gray, and charcoal-gray trousers
with a satin stripe down the outside seam. A white rose
was stuck into his lapel and he was wearing gloves. He
looked even more like a millionaire than he had the

night before, like Fred Astaire singing "Puttin' on the Ritz."

He looked straight at her and crossed his arms. "Well, finally," he drawled. "I've been looking for you for hours."

All eyes turned to her. She felt her face burn as David the married TDH walked toward her and the umbrellas around her and Barry parted like the Red Sea.

Before she could say anything, he had peeled off a glove and held up his left hand. It was naked.

"No ring," he observed, moving his hand this way and that.

Saying nothing, she lifted her gaze from his long fingers to his long car.

"It says 'Just Married,' " she stated flatly.

The sky cracked open; rain poured over both of them as if from a bucket. Barry had cozied his way under the old lady's parasol and was watching the interchange with fascination.

"What," the lady asked him, "she runaway bride?"

"You got me," Barry said. "I'm just living with her for the summer."

The lady's mouth formed an O and her eyes darted from Barry to David and back again. "Ah so," she murmured. "Much confusing excitement."

"I was the best man," David said to Allison. "Honest."

"I'll bet," she tossed at him over her shoulder, trying to find passage to the sidewalk. The brim of her fedora drooped around her head, spigoting water down her collar and raising goose bumps along the slender column of her neck. Tugging at the hat, she shook herself, still negotiating a retreat toward the shelter of the overhang above Tung Fat's. But the other bystanders were pressed shoulder to parasol and didn't seem eager to let her through.

"Please," she said, "I'm soaking wet!" Then, doubling forward, she sneezed so hard, her fedora fell off.

David's brows went up, two bushy Vs above his deep-set eyes. He came forward, retrieved the hat before she could, and popped it back on her head.

"Come on," he said. "Let's go."

Allison blinked. "Go? Where?"

"Your place, I suppose."

Barry brightened. Allison gave a nervous laugh and took a step backward into the sheet of rain. "I'm on a case," she said. "I'm looking for Raphael's dog."

Barry scowled. "Aunt *Al*," he groaned, "are you crazy?"

Ignoring him, she looked at the throngs of people. "Have any of you seen a Shar-Pei recently? I'm authorized to offer a reward for information regarding his whereabouts."

No one spoke. They were too busy tittering and speculating. David just stood beside her and smiled That Smile. He smelled even better than he had the night before, though Allison noted he'd cut himself shaving. There was a minuscule line of red on his otherwise smooth, square jaw. The raindrops caught on the ends of his seal-black hair, clinging to him like the whisper of scent that wafted toward her as he leaned down and took her briefcase from her.

"Come on, Allison," he said, lacing his fingers through hers. Her small hand seemed even smaller as it spread to accommodate his, the rough velvet of his skin wrapping itself around her like a shield against the rain.

"Barry," she called, turning around. He made two victory fists in the air and hurried to catch up with her and David, dodging puddles and the swerve of an angry driver who'd gotten stuck behind the parked Lincoln. Water sliced at him from an angle, but he hopped out of the way with the dexterity one would expect of a guy who called himself "The Human Fly of 'Frisco."

"Traitor," she muttered. "Look, you," she said to David, but apparently he didn't hear her. He was preoccupied with hustling her to the car, tugging on her wrist to keep her going.

She tried to gesture to him, feeling disadvantaged

because of his tremendous height. Straining, she barely reached his chest.

But what a chest. Despite the stiff, formal clothes, she could trace the outline of sculpted pectorals and a flat, taut stomach. She remembered the curly hairs at the base of his throat and had a fleeting vision of what his torso would look like sans the trappings of a fancy church wedding . . . or anything else for that matter.

"Hey!" she shouted, drawing up short. She raised her head to protest, making her face a tempting target for the fat silvery raindrops that pelted her cheeks and forehead like snowballs.

He stopped immediately. "Yes?"

Barry sighed, hugging himself, slouching against the side of the car.

"Uh, this is very flattering," she said, swallowing, "but I'm . . ." Her voice trailed off. She was what? A combination of shyness and exhilaration—and total mystification—was blanking out her brain as it sank in that he had come looking for her. Obviously he'd hurried away from a wedding—whose? his?—without so much as changing his clothes.

David glanced down at her as if from a mountaintop, and put an arm around her shoulders. She could feel the muscles through her sodden clothing, the graze of his fingertips only inches away from her breast. It began to tingle, the nipple to swell against her bra, and she was eternally grateful for the armor of her coat.

"You were saying?" David prompted.

"I was saying," she repeated in a blank, unsteady tone, "I was, uh, I'm busy." She fastened on the words. "I'm on an investigation."

"What a coincidence," he replied, urging her along, molding his hand to her shoulder. "So am I." With his greater bulk, it was easy for him to get her moving again; she'd have to really struggle to prevent him and she didn't want to cause a scene. Not until it was absolutely necessary, anyway.

"Mr. . . . David, come on, please," she said, touching

his hand. She felt him jerk slightly and pulled back as if he had burned her. "This is really nice of you—I think, but . . ."

Nice? David repeated in his mind. She thought he was being *nice*? Didn't she know a hard sell when she saw one? And who was the kid with her? Damn, it couldn't be her son, could it? Only if she'd gotten married when she was eight, he chided himself.

She was saying something to him, straightening her shoulders under the weight of his arm. Without listening, he smiled at her, his gaze roaming over her figure. She was so tiny and compact. Even with that coat on, he knew she had a lovely body, the kind made for caressing and kissing. His flesh awakened at the thought, sending a pleasant frisson up his backbone.

He allowed his fingers to tangle in the tendrils of her hair as they reached the car. They were like wet curls of silk ribbon, smooth and cool.

Evidently she wasn't aware of what he was doing. She was still speaking, and David finally pulled his dazed mind together long enough to hear, "Would you please explain what's going on?"

"Aunt Al, don't screw it up," Barry pleaded. "I'm so cold, I'm about to die."

Ah, *Aunt* Al. No son. Good. He liked things simple.

"I'll explain everything in the car," David said breezily, escorting her to the passenger side of the front seat and opening the door. Barry splashed behind them.

She hesitated. "David, I can't—"

"Look, it's raining cats and dogs"—he grinned—"and you can look for Raphael's pet just as easily from in here as you can tromping around."

"I cannot," she began, but he blithely shut the door.

"You want to sit in the back?" he asked Barry, who nodded in pure and utter gratitude.

David helped him in, ran around to the driver's seat, and slid inside, rubbing his hands. "There, that's better," he said.

The windshield wipers sprang into action and the

heater blew on. David edged into the traffic that had swerved around the Lincoln like buffalo stampeding around an obstacle too big to mow down, and once he'd joined the flow he put his right arm on the back of the seat and smiled at her.

"There's some brandy in the bar behind us," he said. "That ought to warm you up." He pressed a button and the partition that separated them from the rest of the limo whirred down.

"Hey," Barry said from the backseat, snapping his hands away from a cut crystal decanter filled with amber liquid. "Uh, hi, Aunt Al."

"How old is he?" David asked.

"Sixteen," Allison replied, nonplussed by all the luxury. The backseats and floor were a plush blue-gray, with enough space between them and the front seats to put in a tennis court. Directly below her were a TV, a stereo system, and a glistening box that opened with another whirr as David pressed a button.

"There's some Coke and Seven-Up back there too," he said, "if you object to his drinking the brandy." Instantly more decanters filled with clear and dark liquids rose into view, along with a vast array of soda siphons, glasses, and an ice bucket.

And a lacy blue garter—just the kind a bride would wear under a flowing white gown.

"Help yourself," David said. "I think there's some pâté left too. Or caviar, if you prefer."

Barry held up a platter of tiny layered petits fours, iced in pale pink and trimmed with white bells and hearts. "Are you saving these for anything?"

"Barry," Allison murmured. "Please, be polite."

David smiled into the rearview mirror, adjusting it with another switch.

"Help yourself," he told Barry.

Inclining his head in a gesture of thanks, Barry munched on one of the little cakes, swallowed, and reached for another. "Man, this car is cool. It's like something James Bond would own."

"I like technology," David said simply.

"Aunt Al, do you want some of these things?" Barry asked her, reaching for a fourth.

Allison shook her head. "No, thanks," she said stiffly, turning back to David. "And please let us out. I can't look for Bruce Lee in this thing."

David hung one wrist over the top of the steering wheel and gave her a half-smile, which was more than half as devastating as a full one. "Give me a break. You're not really planning to trek around in this weather, are you?"

"Of course I"—her reply was interrupted by a sneeze—"am."

He reached into his breast pocket and pulled out a white silk handkerchief. It was dripping wet. Laughing, he felt for a side pocket stitched into the car upholstery, producing a tissue.

"No way, Allison Jones," he said. "I'm driving you straight home so you can change out of those wet clothes."

"Thank God," Barry said, sighing. He dusted off the empty plate and began filling a glass with ice.

Allison turned her head as she blew her nose, embarrassed by the faint trumpet sound she made. "Listen," she began, but sneezed again.

"No, *you* listen. I'm taking you home and putting you to bed." At his words her head snapped up, and he grinned at her.

"And take off your hat and coat. You're going to catch pneumonia."

"I'm fine," she insisted, hugging herself to keep her teeth from chattering. "And please, don't bother driving me anywhere. I can take a bus."

His eyes widened in mock horror. "A what? You're telling a man driving a limousine you'd rather take a bus?"

Around them, people were waving and honking horns. Two little old ladies in a Cadillac rolled down their windows and blew kisses. David chuckled and blew one back.

"They think we're the ones who got married," he said, waving at the well-wishers.

"That seems to be a problem with you, doesn't it?" she said, tapping her fingers on the armrest. Her heart was hammering in time with the windshield wipers and her breathing was shallow, making her dizzy. She'd never thought to see him again, and he'd come *looking* for her!

Careful, careful, the voice of reason echoed in her ear. Not only is this man a bonfire, he's a forest fire. He is a scorcher.

She glanced at the dashboard, which looked like the instrument panel of a 747, and warmed her hands underneath her arms.

David sighed. "It looks like it's explanation time," he drawled, pressing another button. The glove compartment door opened slowly, unfolding like the drawbridge of a castle. Inside the compartment lay a single object—a large black book with a glossy cover, bearing the title *San Francisco's Most Watchable Bachelors.*

" *'Could they be waiting for YOU?'*" Allison finished aloud.

"Page thirty-five," David said.

"Hey, can I listen to the stereo?" Barry asked, leaning forward.

"Do whatever you want," David said expansively, and closed the partition, effectively sealing Barry in the lap of luxury.

And Allison very near his own lap . . .

She flipped the pages, pausing for a second on page twenty-two: Brian Tulugin, bodybuilder. Then she gazed up at him with her huge blue eyes before she came to the item in question.

"There," he said, taking his hand off the wheel and pointing to the picture of himself. "Read."

He didn't have much on in the photo, just a pair of brief, baggy track shorts and track shoes. His hair was tousled and he was crouching on a rolling lawn, fanning himself with a sweat band.

"Triathlon," he said, pleased that she hadn't gotten past the picture yet. "I won."

"Congratulations," she said automatically, and then her eyes dropped down to the text:

David King, King of the Bachelors! This one's rich, girls—and doesn't mind letting a body know about it. David's a Leo, born in Detroit, Michigan, thirty-two years ago. Cars have been in his karma ever since! After working for five years as a cab driver, David made his move and now he's president of King Limousine Service, the largest limo biz in the Bay Area! David likes "fast cars, slow wine, and hedonistic women." But watch out for him, ladies! He's not the marrying kind! "No way," says the King of the Singles' Scene. "I'd rather drive a cab again." Maybe . . .

She swallowed, tried to think of something to say, and sneezed instead. David handed her another tissue.

"Didn't you get a call from Patricia Courtney this morning?" he asked.

Another trumpet blast. If this kept up, she'd be a hit on moose hunts. She shook her head.

"Damn," he breathed. "Oh, well, I don't suppose I can blame her. She had other things on her mind." He popped a tape into the player above the phone, lowering the volume. Instantly the frenetic beat of heavy rock pulsated through the car.

"Anyway, I just brought that dumb book with me to show you I'm not married."

"And cars are in your karma?" she jeered, crossing her legs. She peeled a strand of lank hair off her forehead, her finger coming away streaked with eye makeup. I must look like the bride of Frankenstein, she thought, trying to check herself in the sideview mirror. Kim Novak would have remembered her umbrella.

"I didn't write that thing," David said, and the tone of his voice made her glance at him.

He was blushing. Against the shimmering silver on the window, his profile was etched as if on glass, two spots of color in his cheeks. His features were rough, sharp, his nose almost too straight and his jaw hard and square. He looked like a tough man who lived hard and played hard, the image softened somewhat by the flush beneath his tan.

Oh, wow, he's not married, she exulted. He's not, he's not, he's . . .

"Let me out," she demanded. "I have work to do."

"Nope. You're in no condition to do anything but sit here beside me."

His tone challenged her. She sat up straight and crossed her arms, wishing the top of his head didn't brush the ceiling. His height overwhelmed her and she didn't like feeling overwhelmed, at least not by him.

Well, maybe just a little.

"Listen, David," she began.

"Not until you have something new to say." When she pursed her lips and stared out the side window, he softened his tone and flattened his hand over her forehead. "I think you're feverish."

"Humph."

"Why are you so jittery?" he asked. "Are you afraid of me?"

"Of course not," she replied quickly, moving her head so that he lost contact with her eyes. Her shoulders hunched as she exhaled. "Look, you're being very nice, and this is all very flattering, but the truth of the matter is, I don't want to get involved with anybody right now." She turned her head to the window to avoid looking at him, unsure of how he would react.

There was a pause. Then he patted her hand.

"That's all right, Allison," he said gently. "I don't want to either."

"Oh." She was abashed. Obviously she'd assumed all this attention he was paying her meant something that it didn't.

"I just thought it might be . . . interesting . . . to get to know you better. You're an unusual woman, Detective Jones."

He picked her hand up and brought it to his lips. His kiss was more like a caress; his eyes peered down at her through those unfairly long lashes.

It might be interesting. Well, that was true enough. But that didn't change her feelings on the matter. Not at all . . .

She inhaled as he ran his dry lips along the back of her hand, turning it over and finishing the kiss on the pulse of her wrist. Tingles fluttered up her arm and circled her breasts, making her nipples peak and harden, her stomach contract.

"I understand how you feel," David went on. "I go out with lots of women who're busy with careers and don't want a heavy relationship with a guy. That's okay with me, Allison. We don't have to swear eternal love to each other. Let's just have some fun. You know, go out now and then. What do you think?"

She pulled her hand away. "I'm not into fun," she told him.

He laughed, taking off her fedora and laying it on the seat between them. "We'll have to change that," he said, signaling for a right turn.

Allison couldn't think of anything else to say. She sat in the wake of the heater, allowing it to dry the hem of her coat, unable to stay annoyed with this man who had, after all, done her a good turn. It would have been miserable slogging through this downpour from the bus stop to her house; she was already beginning to feel a bit feverish. But he didn't have to be so handsome about—er, high-handed about it. And that rock music was giving her a headache.

"That's yours, right? The brown and white one?" he asked, peering through the windshield

Allison looked up, startled. "Yes," she said. "How'd you know how to get here?"

"Every street in this city is imprinted on my brain," he said. "After all, I can't afford to get lost."

"Oh, of course," she said, feeling even more foolish. For a moment she'd supposed he'd looked her street up on a map, or maybe even driven by after the Hubba had closed . . .

He angled the car into her driveway and put on the brake. Allison popped open her door and began to climb out.

"Thanks a lot for the ride," she said too brightly. "Maybe we'll see . . ." Her voice trailed off as he got out and held her door open. Barry, meanwhile, opened his own door and made a dash for the house.

"Use the stairs!" Allison called.

Barry waved a hand to show that he'd heard and disappeared around the back of the house.

"He's got his own place in the attic," she explained. "Now, as I was saying, uh, good-bye."

"You're not getting rid of me that easily," he said, his topaz eyes twinkling with amusement. "And I always see my ladies to the door."

"But I'm not one of your 'ladies,' " she observed. When he didn't reply, she rammed her hat on her head and picked up her briefcase.

"Allow me." David took it from her and cupped her elbow. "Careful. It's slippery."

She smiled wryly, but he didn't catch it as he judiciously led her up the stairs and waited beside the door as she unlocked it. How many times had she walked up these stairs in the rain? And this was the first time she was supposed to notice they were slippery?

Easy, easy, she chided herself. He's trying to be chivalrous. Don't get testy just because you're nervous.

Hesitating, she opened the door and led the way in.

An armada of animals surged toward them—cats and dogs of all sizes running through opened wood doors and down a carpeted flight of stairs. Animals to the left of them and animals to the right of them, thundering toward them until Allison could see the whites of their eyes—if they had whites, and if they had eyes. Allison's menagerie consisted mostly of animals others had rejected because they were less than perfect.

The first to reach her was proud mommy Ironside, loping along on her three legs and carrying a tiny kitten in her mouth. Then came Van Helsing, the Transylvanian hound Allison had rescued from the animal shelter. Squeaks and squawks surrounded them, encouraged by Allison's own silvery laugh as she patted and kissed and greeted her housemates.

"Hello, babies! Miss me?"

David stood by, bemused, laughing as Dirty Harry, Allison's latest mongrel stray, jumped up on his elegant trousers. Then he raised his chin, squinted, and sneezed so loudly that three dust balls of kittens— Mannix, Magnum, and McCloud—scampered away, sliding around the molded baseboards and tumbling over each other in their haste.

"It sounds like you caught something too," Allison said, putting down Gunsmoke, a blind half-Persian, and giving Edward G. Robinson, her tailless dachshund, one last scratch on his tummy. "I'll make you some tea before you go."

"Thanks."

"You can wait in my office," she added, unbuttoning her coat and hooking it over one of the arms of her bentwood hat rack. She plopped her fedora on top and held out her hand for his cutaway.

Instead of taking it off and handing it to her, he caught her fingers and curled them around his. "You're still frozen," he said, "and it's freezing in here."

"I have to watch my bills," she said faintly, trying to draw away. "It costs a lot to heat this place."

"Does it?"

He pulled her toward him, laying a hand on her shoulder as she stumbled on the circular rug that covered the hardwood floor. "Warmer?" he whispered, urging her closer.

Her eyes grew as big as kitten's eyes and she shook her head quickly as she realized what he was doing. He saw her catch her breath, saw the peaks of her nipples through her thin blouse.

"The tea, please," she said, holding herself rigid as his arms came around her. "David, I—"

"Shh," he ordered, pausing on the threshold of the kiss, savoring the anticipation. You could only kiss a woman for the first time once, and he wanted to fulfill the potential that lay in those soft shell-pink lips.

"You—you'll catch my cold," she whispered, her body switching on like a furnace. A wave of heat swept from her toes to her hair and she swayed slightly in his embrace.

"I'll take my chances," he said huskily, and, bending down, pressed his mouth to hers.

Three

Allison tensed, expecting David to bombard her with the passion that was flaring in his eyes. But his kiss was gentle, reassuring, almost courtly, as his satiny lips brushed hers. His mouth was smooth and dry, and he caressed her face with it, his breath soft in the hollow of her cheek, the side of her nose, her forehead.

"Detective Jones," he murmured, nuzzling her temple. The forefinger of his left hand traced the fine curve of her mouth, his touch silky, awakening each nerve to delicate pleasure.

Allison inhaled sharply as he moved lower, to the tension in her neck, his fingers lightly stroking as if he were gentling a frightened animal.

"Stop this," she managed, and he slowly shook his head.

He kissed her again, cradling her head, and her eyes shut tightly as a startled excitement rose over her. Everywhere at once, her body burst into flames—but he gave her nothing to burn with his undemanding, almost affectionate kiss. Instead, the heat built inside her, smoking out everything but the utter delight of him, this stranger who had sought her out like a sleuth on a case—Bogie searching for Ingrid, Jimmy Stewart hunting for Grace Kelly . . .

"Oh, please stop," she murmured. "Oh . . ."

When her lips parted, he kissed the side of her mouth, denying himself the tantalizing victory of penetrating and exploring the sensitive recesses inside. Instead he ran his closed lips under her jaw, trailing up the side of her face to her earlobe, then to the flesh behind it, lifting her hair off her neck.

"Your hair smells like spring rain," he said, burying his face in it. "Ah, lovely Allison."

It excited her to hear him whisper her name. Her hands, pressed against his chest, grew limp and her spine relaxed, his restraint sapping away her resolve.

He supported the back of her neck in one hand and stroked her cheeks and chin with the other, kissing her again, as tenderly as the first time, and the second and the third . . .

Then he pressed his head against the crown of her cap of curls and said lovingly, "Allison, my back is killing me."

She jerked her head up, nearly whapping him in the chin. "I'm sorry!" she blurted out, as if it were her fault that she was so short and he so tall.

And with that, the spell was broken. As if on cue, the animals—who, in some mystical way, had known to settle down and content themselves with watching the two humans kiss—leaped back into action, wagging and barking and mewing and tugging.

"Stop it!" Allison ordered, but Edward G. began maniacally racing around David, stopping every fourth or fifth revolution to yip and dance on his hind legs. Ironside took her kitten back to her nest in the dining room, then trotted out with another one.

And, swooping down the stairs—green, huge, and mighty—Hercule Parrot dive-bombed toward Allison, screaming, "Who done it? Who done it? Rosebud! Cheese, it's the cops!"

"David!" Allison called, waving a warning. The parrot dipped inches above his head, deftly avoided a collision, and roosted in the weathered brass chandelier that was reflected in the mirror on the back of the door.

It was like a scene from Hitchcock's *The Birds.* "Try to make it to my office!" She pointed to the closed door on her right.

He nodded his understanding, hopped over the tan streak that was Edward G., and, shooing Van Helsing out of his way, threw open the gate to escape.

A small yellow elephant blocked his way. Blinking, he took a step back, landing on Ironside's tail. She gave a muffled "Ywlf," not daring to drop her kitten into the maelstrom.

He realized almost as soon as he saw it that the elephant was nothing more than a stuffed toy. Shaking his head, he moved it aside and turned to look for Allison. In his peripheral vision he caught sight of something small and white skittering away from the elephant, and he turned back around just in time to see three white mice racing for a wooden orange crate, a hamster treadmill perched in the middle like a miniature Ferris wheel.

"Go away, now," Allison was saying. "You guys play somewhere else."

Play? David thought to himself. Lord, he'd hate to be around when they were fighting.

"Okay, that's good. Now, you go in here for a while. Good."

The bedlam abated. David heard the sound of several doors being shut and then the click of Allison's boots on the hardwood floor. She walked into the room with the huge green parrot tap-dancing on her shoulder. David winced at the size of the talons pressing into her delicate skin.

But she seemed unperturbed, if a little embarrassed, as she leaned over a wooden perch and cooed to the bird while it wrapped its leathery feet around the dowel and bobbed its head once or twice when she petted its wing.

"Is it always like this?" he asked, running a hand through his hair.

She smiled. "No. Sometimes it's worse."

He said nothing in reply, because he didn't know what to say. He'd used the wrong word when he'd said she was interesting, he thought. The right one was eccentric. A bit demented.

He smiled. Adorable.

"So, tea," she said, and plugged in a hot plate next to her desk. "I have herbal and I have regular—"

"Allison," he murmured, coming toward her, "are you going to pretend it didn't happen?"

"You know, if you reverse your name, it's King David," she said, moving away from him. "But you really should be Goliath, because you're tall and . . ."

"Allison," he remonstrated, his voice tinged with the lingering reminder of his erotic vitality.

Her hand jerked over the sugar bowl. "What?" she asked cautiously.

He said nothing, only sighed.

She sat in the chair behind her desk and folded her hands together. "Do you like my office?"

She was using the cluttered desk as a barrier between them, he realized. She had pulled her chair under it as if she were a rabbit barricading itself inside a hollow tree stump. But it was a line of defense easily penetrated.

To put her at ease, he examined her office. It was decorated in the grand old styles of the twenties and thirties, art nouveau and art deco. An Egyptian table, lacquered black and inlaid with lapis lazuli and turquoise, supported a glass lamp composed of arched lavender tiers. The sensuous curves of art nouveau traced wallpaper lilies and entwining leaves up walls that sported thirties-style plaster heads—a Japanese geisha, a brassy blonde, a harlequin. There were geometric mirrors and odd, square picture frames surrounding posters from old detective movies: *The Maltese Falcon*; *Farewell My Lovely*; *Murders in the Rue Morgue*.

So this was Allison, he thought. A nostalgia buff. And here he was, Mr. Twenty-Second Century. How ironic.

How intriguing.

She was playing back her phone messages. He continued to scan the room, waiting, and he smiled when he heard the breathless voice of Bob's fiancée—oh, man, correct that, his *wife*—struggling to explain that David King was, in fact, not married.

"Honestly, Miss Jones, it really was a joke. They're at the jeweler's now, getting the ring sawed off, and I could kill them both because we're supposed to get married in *one* hour!"

There was a little squeal on the tape. "My dress is here!" she cried. "I've got to go! 'Bye!"

Allison smiled faintly, her face awash with pink. It dusted her cheeks and chin and peeked out from the ringlets that framed her face. She looked like Snow White, David thought, peaches and cream and that black hair. Disney couldn't have done any better.

"Well," she murmured, "that was nice of her."

"And me," he added.

The pink metamorphosed into red. "I'm sorry if I leaped to conclusions. I don't, usually."

"Oh, no?"

Allison said nothing. He perched beside her on the edge of the desk and watched her make the tea. She was nervous. The water spilled over the edge of one hand-painted cup and she made a little face as she set the glazed teakettle down.

"Do you want anything?" she asked, not looking at him, and when he didn't speak, she peered up at him through her lashes.

Redder still, and edging into exasperation, she murmured, "In your tea?"

"No."

He took the cup out of her hand and set it on the desk beside a brass daily calendar. Picking up one of her hands, he cradled it between both of his. The coolness of his monogram ring made a startling contrast to the renewed warmth that began to flood her, and she willed the color from her cheeks as he smiled at her short nails, the ends bitten off. No Jean Harlow glamour here, Mr. King of Bachelors, she thought, mentally drawing in her fingers.

He rubbed her knuckles with his thumb, tracing the

faint lacework of veins on the back of her hand. His fingers moved constantly, as if impatient to feel all there was to feel, caress every part of her she would permit.

"What's this?" he asked, tapping a semicircular scar just above her wrist.

"Recalcitrant client," she murmured, crossing her knees under the desk and clenching her free hand in her lap. "He'd been locked in the pound and he was nervous." That'd been the Case of the Nervous Norwich Terrier.

David caressed the small scar, his grip on her wrist brooking no escape attempts. She felt a wave of empathy with the terrier.

"It looks like it hurt," he said softly. "Your hands are delicate. It wouldn't take very big teeth to take a chunk out of them."

"A couple of stitches. It goes with the territory." She cleared her throat. "Please, let go."

"Hey, *I* don't bite," he murmured.

He leaned forward, examining her face, fingers gliding like silky brands from fingers to lips, outlining their small, soft pinkness with the barest whisper of pressure. He was so close that his breath stirred the raven tendrils that grazed her cheek. His lashes almost brushed against her skin as he scrutinized her, and the back of her neck began to prickle, her spine to liquefy. The delicate scent of his boutonniere blended with his after-shave and the clean smell of rain on his hair, and Allison couldn't help inhaling. Delighting her senses, thrilling her, he loomed tall as he sat on her desk, a huge man; the way he hunched his shoulders as he studied her was at once endearing and awe inspiring.

"No, not a single tooth mark," he went on, turning her face to the light. "You won't need a rabies shot after all."

In spite of herself, she smiled weakly. He looked boyish as he teased her, and he tempted her, but she knew she wasn't ready for what he assumed was going to happen between them.

Yet the thought of it made her dizzy with wanting him.

She removed his hand from her face and brought it down to the desk, then took a deep breath. "David," she began, and the mere voicing of his name made her stop for a moment. She was going to send him away, she thought gloomily, and she got turned on just saying his name. Was this dumb or was it the smartest thing she'd ever done?

"Yes, Allison?" He lifted a strand of her hair and rolled it between his fingers. He was the most tactile, sensuous man she'd ever met. He couldn't seem to get enough of touching, experiencing, savoring.

He moved from a strand to a curl, twining it around his finger. Outside the rain was dancing on the windows, blurring the colors of the room into muted washes and shadows. It gave her face a gauzy, smooth, vulnerable look that made David's throat go dry.

Watch it, King, he cautioned himself. Your predatory nature is being seriously threatened here.

"David, I like you." Her voice was low and husky. In the ensuing silence the animals raised their caterwauling to a fever pitch, demanding their mistress. Allison seemed not to hear it, nor did she stir when something began to hit the door with the force of a small battering ram.

He beamed at her, preparing to move in for a celebratory kiss, but she held up her hand before he could zero in on his appealing target.

"I like you, but I'm really awfully busy and I just don't have much time to—"

"Hey, that's okay," he cut in. "We'll see each other when we can."

He smiled, but inwardly he was thinking, damn, if she was brushing him off, he wouldn't stand for it. Awfully busy. Next week she'd be telling him she couldn't see him because she was shampooing her hair.

He stopped himself. No, this wasn't a brush-off. She was tremendously attracted to him. There was no way she could deny that; he'd felt her shivering in his arms when they'd kissed—and it wasn't because she was cold. Quite the opposite, in fact. He saw the way she studied his body when she thought he wasn't looking. Then why . . . ?

She must have a boyfriend. Hell.

But she hadn't told him that. And if she chose not to mention it, it was because he still had a chance. As long as there was hope, he intended to use every means at his disposal to get to her. He thought of the bed upstairs—that must be where it was, since she glanced up there so often—of all the pleasure they could share, the delight that was lying in wait, as it were. . . .

No. I want more than that from her.

The words were so loud in his mind that he half-stood. In his haste he almost knocked over his teacup; it rattled on the saucer and a few wheat-colored droplets splashed onto the desk.

At the same time the office door burst open and a deluge of creatures poured in. Instantly Edward G. was at the hem of David's trousers, his entire body wagging, instead of the tail he lacked, as he worried the fabric, while Hercule circled the two of them like a plane in a holding pattern.

"Hey," David said, gently shaking his leg and protecting his head at the same time. "Let go, guys."

"Eddie, stop!" Allison cried. Meanwhile Van Helsing did figure eights around her desk and the Egyptian end table, his ferocious tail jeopardizing the future of the glass lamp, which teetered and tottered as if the famous earthquake of 1906 were recurring. The kittens—the M&M&Ms—mewed as if they were laughing at the hubbub.

Allison picked up a few pets and tried to herd all the others toward the door. Edward G. Robinson continued his assault on David's leg. A rooster—David blinked, but yes, it was a rooster—poked its beak in the door, saw the cats, and minced away.

"Edward G., come find your ball," Allison told the dog

as she peeled him off David. Hercule Parrot came in for a landing on her shoulder and tried to bite her ringlets. "Come on, find it! Find it!"

The dog barked and dove out of her hands, nails clattering on the wooden floor as he raced toward the living room. Shooing Hercule away, Allison ran a hand through her hair, revealing a widow's peak on her forehead that gave her the look of a classical, though not very serene, Madonna.

David brought up the rear with the three kittens cradled in his arms. They looked about as big as cotton balls compared to him, and he chuckled as one of them began to bat his thumb.

"Is it time for my scar?" he asked the tiny kitten. "Huh, tough guy? Should I get out my slingshot?" The kitten craned its neck at him and, wide-eyed, began to purr.

Then David grimaced. "Oh, Allison, tell me he's crying," he groaned. He made a face. "He's not."

She shut her eyes. "I'm sorry," she said. "They're not on their best behavior today. I'm trying to get them to go on the paper, but . . ."

He let her take the kittens from him, being especially careful with the one who was least housebroken. She hurried out of the room and, in the next one, he heard her scolding the kitten.

"Naughty Magnum! Bad, bad! We don't go potty on people!"

He washed his hands in the kitchen—nothing had gotten on his clothes—sneezed three times, and ambled into the room where she sat on the floor with the kittens. Her legs were stretched out before her like a little girl as she lectured Magnum. The other two kittens cavorted around her, chasing a spool of thread, bashing into her and toppling over.

"Don't be too hard on the little guy," David said, bending down and patting the offender on his small, fluffy head. "I don't suppose they're used to strangers."

"You're right," she said, not realizing that she was

divulging the fact that she didn't date much—at least not casually. Or else that she never brought them home.

"And you're beautiful." David cupped her chin with his thumb and forefinger. "Has anyone ever told you that?"

"I've heard it a few times," she said honestly. And each of those few times the man who'd murmured those words to her had meant them, she was sure. Each of her old flames had wined her and dined her . . . and eventually things hadn't worked out.

She didn't blame them. There was something about her, she supposed, that made them go. Nothing horrible, nothing dramatic. It was like a mathematical axiom: Men leave Allison Jones.

So, big deal. She had her work and her friends, and she wasn't about to jump into the fray again—especially with a man who had nothing in common with her. Especially with a Most Watchable Bachelor who prided himself on attracting hedonistic women.

Which she was not, she thought. She didn't live in the fast lane. She didn't even live in the middle lane. She lived in the carpool lane, the one for slowpokes, the frontage road that paralleled the highway. She was not a David King playmate type.

Darn.

"Look, let's just go out together now and then," David said, blinking as the phantom rooster peered in, turned around, and strutted away. He had no idea where the rest of the menagerie had disappeared to, though he could hear them, and he wondered briefly how Allison could bear this noise and hysteria all the time.

"No strings, no big commitment," he went on expansively. "You want your freedom, so do I. After all," he added with a wry smile, "I have a reputation to protect."

Mannix had crawled into David's arms and was batting his boutonniere. David sneezed; Allison remembered that they'd left their tea in the other room and thought about adjourning to her office.

But that would just prolong their time together until

the inevitable good-bye. The trouble was, she didn't know how to shorten it. She had a feeling that David King didn't ever take "good-bye" for an answer. Well, there was only one way to find out. . . .

She took a deep breath. "David, good-bye."

He looked at her, a slight frown hardening the angles of his face like the facets on a finely cut diamond. "What did you say?"

Just as she'd thought. Not in his vocabulary, at least not when it was a woman saying good-bye to *him*. It probably worked the other way around.

Without uttering another word, she started to rise. David put Mannix down and took hold of her hands. She was aware that her blouse was still damp and her nipples still jutted through the cloth, and she hunched slightly as she tried to meet his steady gaze, and failed.

"I have some things to do," she said. "I appreciate the ride home, but—"

"Allison," he said firmly, "I'm going to see you again."

Her shoulders sagged and she hunkered down still further. "David, I just can't—"

She was interrupted by the sound of a key in the lock of the front door.

"It's just *moi*, Ally-cat!" a woman's voice trilled. "Are you *chez*?"

Allison rolled back on her heels. David got to his feet first and helped her up, hands lingering around her waist. His arms brushed the sides of her breasts and he smiled at her, his dark, deep-set eyes filled with a confident intensity that made her feel as though she were standing on the edge of an impossibly high cliff, then falling, falling . . .

"Hey, Allison, where are—?"

Her best friend, Janet, sailed around the corner and came to a standstill at the threshold.

"Oh, excuse *me*," she chirruped, posing in an exaggerated stance of abject embarrassment. Her platinum hair was wound into braids that crowned her head, and her blue eyes fluttered ridiculously at David. "I'm charmed, I'm sure," she said, tossing a thick scarf over her shoulder as she strode forward to shake David's hand. Piano keys were knitted along the edge of the scarf; above each octave were the words "You tickle my ivories." Rainbow suspenders crossed a white thermal underwear T-shirt, and black jeans and ballet slippers completed her ensemble.

"Janet Madison, David King," Allison said. "Janet's a mime down at the Cannery."

"Among other things," Janet cut in. "I'm also a professional tooth fairy." She looked at Allison. "Hey, I can come back later if I'm interrupting anything." Twinkling eyes glittered at David and she couldn't hide a mischievous grin.

"Actually, David was just leaving," Allison said quickly. "So we can go after all."

"Go . . . ?" Janet echoed, looking blank. Allison clenched her teeth at her and she instantly recovered. "Oh, right. To that place we were going to. Good."

David suppressed a rueful grin at the obviousness of Allison's ploy to get rid of him. "I have to be taking off anyway," he drawled, finally letting go of her.

But I'll be back, his look told her. Count on it.

Swallowing, trying not to acknowledge the unspoken words, Allison walked him to the front door. Janet followed, eyes agog.

"Good-bye," she said again, feeling a twinge of regret. Maybe she was being stupid, she thought. He was so nice, and handsome, and talk about a great kisser . . .

"See you later," David replied pointedly. He bobbed his head at Janet and began to walk toward his limo. There was a huge crowd around it.

Allison hadn't quite shut the door when Janet started in. "Wow, what a hunk!" she exclaimed. "Oh, Ally-cat! Where on earth did you find him?"

Listening on the other side, David grinned at Allison's response. "In a bar in North Beach."

"You're kidding!"

"I was on a case," Allison said. "Looking for an animal."

"Well, from the looks of him, I'd say you found one."

David beamed as he stood listening on the porch. This was getting interesting, he thought. Maybe that woman would talk some sense into her.

"And I thought you only had eyes for Hunter," Allison was saying.

"Oh, well of course I do!" her friend blurted out. "I'm so madly in love, it gives me gas. But it sure is nice to window-shop now and then. And that guy of yours fills a whole window."

"Well, thanks," David murmured under his breath. He cast a concerned glance at the crowd around the limo. They were getting brave, hands hovering above the door handles. But this eavesdropping was too good to miss.

"He's not my guy," Allison insisted.

Then again, maybe it wasn't.

"Oh? That's not the impression I got when I walked in. Things looked pretty cozy. Oh, Al, he's got such *big* hands!"

"Janet, give me a break. You know who he is? He's in that bachelor book. Do I need a guy like that?"

"I think that's exactly what you need. Just somebody to have some fun with. You don't have to marry him, for heaven's sake."

His thoughts exactly. David blew Janet a mental kiss, then grimaced as a teenage boy tried the front door of the limo. Time to go.

"I know I don't have to marry him," Allison retorted. "I don't want to marry him. I don't want to marry anybody!"

"All right, everybody," David said calmly as he strode down the walkway to the Lincoln. "Please leave the car alone."

Though most of them backed away, a small old woman kept her post by the tinted windows. "Where's the bride?" she demanded. "Where's the bride?"

He almost said, "Inside the house," intending it to be a joke.

But at the mere thought, he broke into a sweat. Allison, a bride? Allison, his . . .?

Will you stop this nonsense? he chided himself. One guy gets married and you lose your cool. You need to get some perspective on this thing.

Besides, Allison didn't want to get married. She'd said so herself.

That was good. That made her safe. Women who wanted unthreatening, casual relationships were getting scarce in the city. Among his ladies, the desire to get married was reaching epidemic proportions. He needed a reasonable woman like Allison Jones to share the joys of bachelorhood with.

"Where's the bride?" the old lady demanded.

"I haven't got one," he said, dazzling her with That Grin.

Her face lit up. "Oh? Well, I've got a niece, such a nice girl."

"I'm sure you do." He smiled again and scooted around to the driver's side.

"She's fascinating!" the old lady cried. "She's got a job!"

He waved at her as he shut the door and turned on the engine. The woman was still speaking, but he cranked up his tape and leaned back into the blast of heavy metal rock.

As he pulled away, he glanced at Allison's house just in time to see a neon light flicker on in the window. It was a huge lavender eye surrounded by the words "Allison Jones, Pet Detective" and her phone number.

She was fascinating. She had a job. She didn't want to get married.

"Allison, you're my kind of woman," he said as he eased the gas pedal to the floor and drove away from the curb. "And I'll prove it to you."

Well, he'd believed he'd prove it to her, David thought

morosely as he hung up the phone. He was cruising in his 1957 Rolls Royce Silver Wraith, a honey of a car with smooth leather seats, crystal ornaments, hand-carved wood trim, and heaven under the hood. He turned the wheel with his forefinger, savoring the car's exceptional handling. It was certainly more responsive than a certain Miss Allison Jones.

"What is it with her?" he asked himself out loud in the rearview mirror. "Is she made of stone?"

If so, he figured he'd done everything he could to wear down her rough edges—flowers at dawn and sunset, phone calls, a limo and chauffeur parked outside her house twenty-four hours a day.

But a week had gone by and she never returned the phone calls and she didn't use the limo. According to his sources, she was still taking the *bus.* At least she'd kept the flowers.

He grinned. The inside of her house must look like a funeral parlor by now.

The grin faded. He almost felt as if *he* were in a funeral parlor. Dammit, he missed her, missed her compelling blue eyes, the mixture of tough private eye and soft, huggable woman. He missed the fun he thought they were going to have together.

He pursed his lips in a frustrated pout. He missed all these things and he hardly knew her. It was a new thing to him to miss a woman this much. New, and potentially dangerous.

"So why are you looking for her, King?" he demanded as the phone whirred. He grabbed the receiver in a flash.

"Kemo sabe? Possible sighting on Grant," his dispatcher, Tex, announced. "Carlos is following a lady with a fedora and a gray coat."

Bingo, David thought. Unconsciously, he pulled at his shirt sleeves and adjusted his tie. He was wearing a navy blue three-piece suit, a white shirt, a sedate blue and burgundy tie, and new Italian loafers that shone on the gas and brake pedals. He had broken a blind date to go a-hunting for Allison, one that Bob had set up before whisking his bride off to Hawaii. "I'm going to marry you off this year if it kills me, King," he'd told David. And what red-blooded bachelor could resist a woman whose nickname was Rosie the Riveter?

"Okay, I'm on my way," David said, and his stomach contracted unaccountably as he hung up.

I am not nervous, he told himself. It was just the thrill of the chase.

And the other half of him said, Right, King. Right.

Allison clutched Bruce Lee against her chest and scowled at the man in the sunglasses and satin baseball jacket. Behind them, the police had barricaded the north end of Kearny with sawhorses to prevent the crowds from rushing in. Waving above them like a robot dinosaur, a cranelike affair sprouted three fins which turned out to be two men and a movie camera.

"I tell you, this is the missing pet of a client," Allison insisted for the thirtieth time. "This dog is *not* public domain."

"Lady, he was just nosing around the garbage cans," the man in the satin jacket said tiredly, also for the thirtieth time. Emblazoned across the back of his jacket were the words "Kung Fu Karnival" and below that, "Rocko Davis, Assistant Director."

"Finders keepers," the man went on, holding his hands out for the dog.

Bruce Lee was spectacularly ugly in Allison's eyes. Who could understand why a dog would be bred for the folds of skin that drooped beneath his eyes and muzzle? But he was Raphael's beloved—and expensive—little China doll, and she didn't care if this Hollywood know-it-all had decided he was "vital" for the next scene. He was not going to scamper into a burning papier-mâché pagoda.

"Come on, lady," Rocko growled. Bruce Lee growled back.

So did Allison. "No."

At that moment David walked up behind Allison and put a hand on her shoulder, nearly startling her out of her skin.

She whirled around. Her lips parted and she blinked, then caught her lower lip between her teeth like a guilty child. Ah, Allison, David thought, where have you been all my high-gloss life?

"Hi," he said easily. "Running into some trouble?"

Rocko Davis looked from one to the other. "What're you, her brother?"

David chuckled. He supposed they did resemble each other in hair and coloring, though of course the eyes were different. And then, there was the height thing . . .

"Yeah," David drawled. "I'm dominant and she's recessive."

The man frowned. "Listen, I don't care about your sex life. I just need that dog."

Allison groaned. "He was talking about genes. You know, as in biology? I'm short, he's tall. I have blue eyes, he has brown."

"I'm wearing a suit, you're wearing a trench coat," David finished easily, as if he were making sense.

Rocko screwed up his face. "I don't get it."

"I've found Bruce Lee," Allison said to David. "He won't let me keep him. He wants him to run into a burning building."

Rocko scowled at her. "A miniature pagoda. There's no collar or any kind of identification. As far as I'm concerned, this is just some Chinatown mutt."

"Mutt!" Allison cried. "This is someone's pet!"

"Pet, schmet. He's a prop." He eyed her. "You can't prove anything, anyway."

David cleared his throat. "Allison, dear, may I speak to you a moment?"

It took her a few heartbeats to respond. How had he found her? she wondered. He must think she was incredibly rude, not returning his calls. And those fancy cars! Barry was about to crucify her for not letting him ride around in them. Maybe she should. Maybe she should send him onto the streets to keep him out of trouble.

She sighed. Last night she'd peeled her recalcitrant nephew off the side of the Palace of Fine Arts. "But I'm halfway up!" he'd pleaded.

"You're also halfway down," she'd pointed out. "Please complete the trip." She figured he had a great future as an urban window washer. Maybe he could work his way up—start in San Francisco and achieve the pinnacle of his career in New York City. Maribeth—and the grandparents—would be so proud. . . .

"Allison?" David urged.

Head bent, scratching Bruce Lee under the chin, she nodded to show that she'd heard. David gestured to her to step a little away so they could confer in private. In the distance someone shouted "Quiet on the set!" through a megaphone and everybody froze in mid-action.

Except Bruce Lee, who barked. And David, who murmured, "I can get the dog away from him, but it's going to cost you."

"Lights!" yelled the megaphone man.

"How?" she asked, holding Bruce Lee's mouth shut. He squirmed in her arms and she was glad she had to pay attention to him—anything to avoid David's probing gaze. Her heart was hammering and her palms were sweating. Maybe she was getting distemper, she thought. Janet kept saying she was being an idiot. "He turns you on, you turn him on. Honestly, Ally-cat, is there anything wrong with pure, unadulterated sex appeal? Don't let a hunk like that go to waste, for Pete's sake!"

"How?" she repeated when she realized that David hadn't answered her. He was staring at her, mentally undressing her, and she clutched Bruce Lee to her bosom as a shield against the laser-hot eyes.

"Camera!" bellowed the megaphone man.

"Leave that to me," David replied.

"What's the price?" She turned her back to Rocko, who was hovering nearby and straining to hear their conversation. In spite of the fact that she alternately wanted to sink through the asphalt and soar beyond the camera crane, the entire interaction reminded her of the passport scene in *Casablanca*.

"Dinner," David said. "Tonight."

She hesitated for a moment before she nodded in agreement, finally meeting his eyes. Hers were glittering aquamarines, and David felt his chest tighten with appreciation and desire.

"All right, you're on," she whispered.

"Action!" yelled the megaphone man, and David's face broke into a huge, satisfied, expectant grin.

Action, he thought. All right.

Four

David smiled politely at the elderly policeman as he, Allison, and Bruce Lee walked through the barricades toward David's Rolls. An eager young officer had offered to guard the Silver Wraith while David went to find Allison, and he looked genuinely disappointed to see the car's owner.

Tromping beside David, finding it difficult to keep up with his long stride, Allison was sizzling.

"*I* was going to tell Rocko I'd bring in the cops if he didn't cooperate," she grumbled. "I was trying to avoid making a scene." Her arms were beginning to ache. Bruce Lee was not a little dog, and he was antsy. On top of that, he wasn't at all grateful for having been rescued. Neither was she, since David had done nothing she wasn't capable of.

David gave her a comforting pat on the shoulder and immediately slowed his pace. "But you've got the dog, haven't you? That's all that matters."

"But now I've been shanghaied into dinner," she blurted out, and realized how rude that sounded. "I'm sorry," she said quickly, shifting Bruce. "It's just that . . ."

David let her words trail off. It's just that you're a nervous wreck, he silently told her. He quickly decided not to bother with the dinner reservations he'd been about

53

to make. Rosie the Riveter may have been ripe for a secluded little table with soft lights and violins, but this was not Allison's day for heavy one-to-one interaction. Any fool of a bachelor could see that.

"Are you sure you don't want me to carry the dog for you?" he asked.

She shook her head. "No, thanks." Her tone was less brittle. "It took me so long to find him, I want to make sure I still have him when I get to Raphael."

"I can call for somebody to take him over to the Hubba," he suggested, helping her into the car. He grimaced at the dog, remembering Mannix's little accident, and sent a prayer to V-8, the god of sports cars, to spare the wood trim and meticulously cared-for leather seats. As he shut the door and walked around to the driver's side, he decided that he now had two nervous wrecks on his hands—three, if Bruce Lee didn't like riding in cars.

The first thing David did when he slid behind the wheel—gracefully, Allison noted, as if he were born to it—was pick up his phone, dial a number, and say, "All clear. Mission accomplished."

He laughed at something the person on the other end of the line said and hung up. Then the car began to purr and David made a smooth turn to the right.

Allison looked at him, suspicion darkening her eyes to sapphire. "What mission?"

David shrugged. "I had an errand to run, that's all."

"What errand?"

Three teenage girls in a Volkswagen Beetle roared up beside them and began to giggle and wave. One of them rolled down her window. David rolled down his.

"Bitchen car!" she yelled, and the driver revved her engine.

David flashed them The Grin and they began to fall to pieces.

Exhaling, Allison looked away, wondering if blushing was another symptom of distemper, along with clammy paws and heart palpitations. All three seemed to be recurring with alarming frequency. Like malaria.

David chuckled at the admiring teenyboppers, then popped a tape in and settled back in his seat. The music was loud, wild, young. He saw the frown on Allison's face and immediately turned it down.

"So, here's the plan," he said, peering at her. Her skin was almost translucent, like alabaster, except for the high color on her cheeks and forehead. He started to lose himself in staring at it, aware that he had to keep his attention on the road, but somehow feeling compelled to examine every flawless inch of her face.

She turned back from the window and caught him staring at her. Heat again washed over her face, and her first thought was, He makes me feel as pretty as Myrna Loy.

Well, of course he does, dum-dum. He's the King of the Bachelors. It's his job.

"The plan," he said slowly, "is to drop off the dog, then I'll put you into a limo and come back for you in an hour. Deal?"

"What errand?" she asked, shaking herself. "How did you know where to find me?"

"I looked all day," he said soulfully. "You don't know the trouble you've caused me."

"*I've* caused *you*," she began, then smiled faintly. "Thank you for all the flowers. They're beautiful. My house looks like the Grand Hotel." Complete with guests, who crowded around the limos day and night. Allison was now the object of intense neighborhood speculation. Mr. Scarpare, who lived three doors down, wanted to know "Which horse? Which race?"

He touched her hand. "Why didn't you return my calls?"

His skin was warm, his fingers long as they wrapped around hers. Because of this, she said to herself as a few thousand megawatts of pleasure jolted through her. Because I don't want to surrender to the desire to let you into my world.

"David," she said, "please. You can have any woman you want, so—"

"That remains to be seen, doesn't it?" he murmured, and gave her hand a squeeze.

The fedora cast a shadow above her eyes, but he could tell she was knitting her brows. The dog yipped and she pulled her hand away to hold him, fussing with him for a few seconds before she replied.

"I told you already, I don't want to get involved with anybody."

David nodded impatiently. "And I told you, neither do I." Suddenly he broke free of the traffic and screeched to the side of the street into a bus zone where the sign clearly said No Parking Anytime.

"Allison, Allison," he murmured, shaking his head. "What am I going to do with you? Listen, I promise you I won't make more demands on you than you're prepared to accept."

"You already have," she pointed out.

He appraised her. "Ha. I can read people pretty well, Ally-cat, and you're not sending out 'go away' signals. Not by a long shot."

She would not blush, she told herself. She would not.

"Listen, trust me. I won't start demanding all your time. I'm not that kind of guy. You can carry on with your life the same as you always have. All I'm asking for is to get to know you."

She looked at him. "To what purpose?"

The sun was beginning to set. Streaks of fire coursed across the sky, casting David's face in a glow of muted crimson. Scarlet blazed in his eyes and she found herself gripped by the desire to have him kiss her. It was like a sudden, living thing, this wanting. Electricity filled the car, jittering and vibrating around and within her. Even the dog must have sensed it, for he calmed down in her arms and lay quietly, as if waiting for something.

"Do we have to have a reason?" David breathed, his

pupils dilating. He leaned toward her and pressed his closed mouth against hers.

Her head tipped backward, slowly falling against the back of the seat as David nipped her upper lip, then slid the tip of his tongue down the arch of her neck. He gathered her up in his arms, mindful of the dog, and caressed her shoulders. Feeling her tension, he moved his hands around her upper arms and kneaded them, delineating the taut muscles and easing out the knots.

"Feel better?" he murmured, moving to her upper back.

She nodded. "Yes and no."

"Well, that's honest," he said, finishing off his massage with a light, sweeping stroke across her collarbones before he moved back behind the wheel. Behind him, a bus loomed large, honking, and David blithely waved in the rearview mirror and pulled away from the curb.

After making some calls on the car phone, David located Raphael at his apartment in Castro Gulch. He lived above a men's beauty salon called The Strap, and Allison was delighted to discover that he, too, had an interest in the thirties. He had a marvelous collection of Depression era glass.

But at the moment, Raphael was more interested in his reunion with Bruce Lee than in discussing the charms of rainbow-hued plates and vases.

"Daddy's baby!" he cried, weeping, cradling the dog in his arms. "Bruce Lee, you are the naughtiest little thing!"

The dog was having a field day with Raphael's chin, licking it wildly, squirming in his "daddy's" arms with unrestrained joy.

"Oh, Detective Jones," Raphael said, squeezing Allison's hand, "I don't know how to thank you!" He wiped away his tears. "Well, of course I do. Let me get my checkbook."

Allison smiled, retaining her composure, though empathetic tears of happiness welled in her eyes. It wasn't until she and David had left the apartment that she allowed herself a few sniffles while she folded the check and put it into her purse.

"You old softie," David said, putting his arm around her. "That meant a lot to you, didn't it?"

She made a halfhearted attempt at shrugging off his arm, then sighed and dabbed at her eyes with his proffered handkerchief. "Yes, it did. It just kills me when I can't find somebody's pet." She made a face. " 'Finders keepers,' my foot! I'd have punched Rocko out before I'd have given Bruce Lee up to him!"

"Lucky thing you let me handle it, Goliath," David observed. He tousled her hair under the brim of her fedora.

"I think your male chauvinism's showing," she retorted.

"I think your female tenderheartedness is, too," he said, catching the last of her tears with his finger.

She bristled. "Just because I let my feelings show—" she began, but he cut her off with a quick kiss.

"Let's have some fun tonight," he said brightly. "I think we both deserve it."

"But why not? What's wrong with having fun?" Janet asked, flopping on her stomach at the foot of Allison's brass bed.

Allison pulled off the leather pants Janet had offered to lend her. They were not her thing. She folded them on top of Janet's vermilion poncho, which was also not her thing. That left her in tea-colored panties and a matching lace bra, and that just wasn't enough to spend the evening in.

"He's so darn rich," she muttered to herself. "He'll probably expect me to sweep down the stairs in a Bill Blass original."

"That's why I suggested the eccentric look," Janet said, rolling over on her stomach and spreading her Gypsy skirt. She wore ribbons in her hair and earrings two miles long in her earlobes.

"I'm not an eccentric type, either." Allison stood in front of her closet, which was surrounded by wicker stands of roses, irises, and chrysanthemums, and held out her hands, shivering in her underthings.

Hercule Parrot, preening himself as he walked tightrope-style over the the curlicues of the headboard, looked up and croaked, "Play it, Sam! Play it, Sam!" Under the bed, the M&M&Ms mewed and frolicked. Downstairs, on the radio, the evening animal symphony was in full swing.

Janet laughed, plucking a daisy from a vase on the nightstand and pulling off the petals one by one. "No, you're not eccentric, Allison."

Allison ran a hand through her hair, remembered that she'd finally managed to get all the curls going in the same direction, and bit her thumbnail instead. She shifted her weight to her hip as she went through her closet again, her bare feet growing cold on the chilly hardwood floor.

"All I have are sweaters, blouses, jeans, and sweaters." She groaned. "Maribeth's been after me to buy more clothes."

"Maribeth can afford them."

Allison arched a dark brow above a light blue eye. "As my mother is fond of pointing out, so could I, if I'd just grow up and get a decent job."

"Don't grow up," Janet said. "I tried it once. It was terrible."

The bell rang downstairs. Allison's mouth dropped open.

"The cur is early."

Janet scrambled to her feet. "Not to worry, Madame X. *Moi* shall distract him—but not *too* much," she added, giggling.

Allison sighed. "Why am I so nervous?"

" 'That's the glory of, that's the story of—' "

"Janet," she said sharply, "I'm not in love with him. I never could be, either."

"Why not?" Janet demanded, slipping on a pair of clogs.

"We're too different, for one thing."

"Then just have some fun with him." She covered her mouth in a theatrical gesture, miming the dawning of understanding. "Ah, but I have forgotten. You don't want to have fun. We have come full circle. Time to exit, stage right."

She bounded out of the room. Allison, huddling at the open closet, heard her tripping down the stairs, trilling, "Yes, yes, yes! Here I come!"

The front door opened. "Well, hello," Janet said, then bellowed, "Jeans are fine, Ally-cat!"

"Thanks," Allison muttered, rolling her eyes toward the ceiling.

But jeans *were* fine. David himself was wearing them with a madras shirt that brought out the gold in his dark honey eyes. They molded his small hips and triathlon thighs, tapering over knees and well-formed calves. As he guided his car—yet another stunner, a flashy red Lamborghini Miura—across the Golden Gate Bridge and over dark roads lined with redwoods and tall pines, shadows flitted across his legs, accentuating the muscles beneath the rough fabric. Each time he shifted, Allison stole a peek, fascinated by the strength emanating from his body.

They didn't speak much; they couldn't. "This car isn't tops in luggage space or noise level," he told her before she fastened her seat belt. "But she'll do one hundred eighty miles per hour on a flat stretch of land."

Now, as they wound around hills and skirted valleys, Allison was deeply grateful for the absence of flat stretches.

"We're just about there," David bellowed in her ear. The car roared to a halt with the grace and precision of the space shuttle, without a trace of whiplash.

"Just wait here a minute," he said as he put on the brake. Then he reached behind his seat, drew out a bundle, and climbed out of the bucket seat. Allison was certain she heard a breathy "heh heh" as he shut the door.

He reappeared half a minute later, dressed almost identically to her: Over his jeans and shirt he wore a gray trench coat, and on his head a black fedora was tilted at a rakish angle.

"What do you think?" he asked. "Oh, here, take this." He handed her a magnifying glass. "And this," he added. Hunkering down into a near crouch, he pinned a red carnation on her lapel.

Then he pinned one on his lapel and held up a second magnifying glass.

"What on earth is going on?" Allison asked as he linked arms with her and urged her up a dark path. Their shoes made muffled crunching noises on the forest underbrush; above them, the moon peered through boughs that rustled in the breeze.

"Elementary, my dear Jones. We're going to a costume party."

She pulled back. "What? You said we were going out to dinner!"

His shrug was little-boy innocent, big-boy mischievous, and his man-size shoulders were accentuated by the buttoned epaulets of his coat. His face was shrouded to his chin, which was square and hard, giving him a mysterious air. She thought of Philip Marlowe, the California shamus, and suppressed a grin. David was he, brought to life in the moonlight.

"There'll be a buffet," he told her. "Come on. You'll have fun."

There was that word again. She huffed. "All right. But next time—" She cut herself off. Who was to know if there'd be a next time?

He laced his fingers through hers and brought her hand to his lips, forcing her to rise on tiptoe.

"Next time, I'll warn you in advance. Tonight I just wanted to surprise you."

Her hand was on fire. You have surprised me, believe me, she thought. You continually surprise me.

"C'mon, Rosebud," he said in a low Bogie voice. "I'm starving."

Crickets were chirping in the bushes, creating a counterpoint to the party noises that grew louder as David led Allison through the overgrown path. His coat looked brand-new, as did his fedora, and she wondered if he'd gone out and bought them solely to pull this prank. She saw a flash of white teeth as he minced toward a large redwood gate, a brilliant smile that told her how much he was enjoying himself. His enthusiasm was infectious, and, despite the fact that she was nervous about meeting his friends, she found herself smiling, too.

The gate creaked open and David motioned her through.

"You go first," he whispered. "There may be guard dogs."

"Thanks," she said dryly.

He took her arm again and led her up a flight of stone steps. "I do a lot of work for these people," he said. "They like to entertain." He checked his watch. "In fact, I should have about a dozen cars and valets out front right now."

She was startled. "Here?"

He nodded. "We're coming in the back way." At her questioning glance, he added, "I like to be unpredictable."

He ushered her through another gate, and she stepped through to a panorama of wealth and opulence that made her catch her breath.

A huge pool shimmered beneath Chinese lanterns, and around it sheiks and princesses, pirates and cancan girls milled and laughed and drank champagne. A band was playing on a platform at one end of the pool, and way down in the distance, at the other end, she saw miles of tables laden with ice sculptures and chafing dishes, attended by men in tuxedos.

Beyond that, a gently sloping lawn edged with oleanders rolled toward a huge, modern redwood house that looked like an art museum. It was split into several levels, the whimsical angles punctuated by both clear round windows and square stained glass windows. Emperors and Coneheads perched like splendidly colored parrots on various wooden balconies. Above them all, huge, ancient trees dropped vines and creepers like knobby curtains around a theater set.

What a perfect setting for a murder mystery, Allison thought, reducing her ritzy surroundings to terms she could relate to.

"Dinner is served," David said, and together they walked toward the tables.

She shrank at his side, feeling horribly outclassed. Not even Maribeth and her surgeon husband attended bashes like this. And certainly not in jeans and trench coats. As she glanced furtively at the other merrymakers, she saw that their costumes were custom-tailored outfits of silk and satin and velvet.

"David, darling!"

A woman's voice rose above the laughter and tinkle of glasses, and Allison heard David murmur, "Oh, damn." Then he smiled brightly and turned in the direction of the voice.

The woman was dressed as a princess of some other century; Allison didn't know which. Her own interest in the past went back no more than fifty or sixty years. But she was fascinated by the cantilevered effect of the woman's costume—tight silk molded an impressive bustline with no apparent means of support. It seemed to be defying gravity. Maybe she's stuck it on with Crazy Glue, Allison thought. She could have a smashing career at the Club Hubba Hubba.

Lady Delilah—soon to be, perhaps, Godiva—was clearly out to kiss him, but in a smooth maneuver David prevented her at the same time that he drew Allison forward.

"Corinne Sanders, this is Allison Jones," he said pointedly.

Allison endured Corinne's appraisal, feeling as glamorous beside her as a little gray pigeon. Stiletto nails, lacquered heels, Allison thought wistfully. Mata Hari goes to Hollywood. She'd get the female lead in a James Bond film any day.

So what? she demanded of herself. You don't care about David. He's not the man who makes your existence on earth a little bit of heaven. Let her fawn all over him. Let her kiss him. That's the kind of woman you expect him to be with anyway. She's only confirming your worst fears. Is that any reason to contemplate pushing her into the swimming pool?

"We were about to get some food," David told Corinne. "It was nice running into you like this." He turned to Allison. "Afterward, we should—"

She wasn't paying attention. She'd gone pale, and was scrutinizing someone across the rows of tables.

"Ally-oop?" he murmured. "Are you okay?"

She roused herself. Damn, but that man across the way looked just like Kevin Krincoulus, an old flame. He was another of the drifters, someone who'd just stopped calling for no apparent reason.

She wilted still further. Axiom: Men leave Allison Jones. Fact: David King was very much a man. Conclusion . . .

Allison Jones, get your fanny out of here.

"I'm okay," she said, touching the brim of her fedora. "I guess I'm pretty hungry."

"I like women with appetites." He took off his hat, his smile growing as his features came into view. He looked as cocky as Errol Flynn. "I like them hungry."

She pretended not to catch his double meaning. "Then you've got the right woman," she replied, resolutely picking up a plate.

He took it from her. "I'll serve you," he said, touching her back. "Just tell me what you want, and how much."

They regarded each other. "A little of everything," she said slowly.

He nodded. "Whatever you want, Allison. I'll get it for you."

Yeah, I'll bet, she thought, and wondered why suddenly she felt like crying

They ate an exquisite meal of poached salmon and rare beef and a million other things that all tasted like sandpaper to Allison. As she sat beside David on a wrought-iron love seat, a troupe of gorgeous women paraded past, making obeisance to The King, who took it all in stride. Allison's smile was firmly in place, but she knew she was failing miserably in the competition between her and the Ziegfeld Follies.

She met the host and hostess—both utterly charming and friendly—and a few men friends of David's who pretended not to notice her lack of high chic. She felt as if she were Doris Day and had stumbled onto the set of *Cleopatra.*

David left her for a moment to ferret out French pastries and champagne. She sat alone on the love seat, legs pressed together at a right angle to her body, hands folded primly, consoling herself with the thought that, at this moment, Raphael and Bruce Lee were probably eating their first meal together in a long time.

And Barry and the side of some high-rise were probably meeting for the first time.

She sighed. What should she do with him? Barry was up to dangerous things, though Maribeth had ridiculed Allison's fears when she'd called long distance again, this time from Spain.

"Humph," Allison said aloud. Maribeth wasn't the one who'd had to pick him up at the police station or watch him snake up the side of her house. When she got back from Europe, they were going to have a nice little chat about Barry's "acting out." If he lived that long.

David had found the pastries and was sailing back with them when he saw the glum expression on Allison's face. Damn, another tactical error, he thought. She's not having a good time.

He set the plates and glasses on the side of a sparkling bronze fountain and ambled over to her. Pulling out his detective's magnifying glass, he peered through it at her and pronounced, "On your feet, Jones. The game's afoot!"

She laughed, startled. "What?"

"In the parlance of the young, we're splitting," he said, helping her to her feet. "So pass out your business cards now if you need to."

"I don't need to," she murmured, embarrassed. As she had thought. He wasn't comfortable having her here as his guest. She wasn't mingling properly and she hadn't had a real manicure since she'd gone to Maribeth's graduate school commencement ceremony three years ago. She looked down at her nails, bitten to the quick, and stuffed her hands into her pockets.

"Then let's go," he said jauntily, throwing an arm over her shoulders.

She assumed he meant he was taking her home, but as he tore along the roads, she saw that he was heading for the city.

"What now?" she asked, clutching the seat with white knuckles.

"Now is just the two of us," he replied, rubbing her cheek with the back of his hand. "I'm sorry the party bored you," he added. "I thought we should make an appearance."

We? She said nothing, confused by his choice of the word. Since when were they a "we"? Had he used "we" the way royalty did: "We shall have a bath tonight"?

David, too, was confused by what he'd said. We? he thought. He wasn't into "we." Why had he said that? What was she thinking about it?

He didn't want to scare her away. Here was the first independent woman he'd met in a long time—one who simply wasn't interested in a long-term relationship—and he certainly didn't want to blow it by acting as if he did.

So watch it, King, he warned himself. Stay light with this lady. She doesn't go for heavy stuff.

There. That was simple enough. He revved the engine, tapping his fingers on the wooden steering wheel.

Beside him, Allison's head was turned toward the window as she watched the landscape. His chest tightened and it was all he could do to keep from making a right at the next fork, which would eventually land the Lamborghini at his doorstep.

Damn, he thought, passing the fork by. If it was simple enough, why did he still feel confused?

Fisherman's Wharf was as light as David could get. In the summertime it was a festival of smells—salt air and steaming shellfish, fresh-baked sourdough bread, beer and popcorn. Tourists milled around, trailing odors of tired perfume and chocolate, from the day's excursion to Ghira delli Square to watch the huge chocolate vats bubbling like mud pots. The locals were huddled in espresso cafes and lace-fringed dollhouses like Allison's, munching fennel-spiced pizza.

"What a view," Allison murmured as she and David strolled along the boardwalk. Spread before them, past the lights of Tarantino's and other restaurants, floated the huge expanse of fluorescent black that was the bay, frosted with silver crests and ruby beacons.

"Yes, a great view." David's voice was soft as he put his arm around her. It felt warm against the chill night air, permeating her a bit at a time until the intrusion became a comforting presence. Her hip brushed his thigh, her trench coat moved against his jeans, and she was aware that only thin pieces of fabric shielded their bare flesh from each other.

The moon shone above them, casting blue-black highlights into David's hair. His eyes were unreadable, shaded, but she could feel the fullness of their gaze upon her. His arm tightened and they stood still, watching the fog wash the scene as it traveled in from the ocean in billowing clouds of ethereal mist. Foghorns sighed. The lights grew softer, ringed by coronas of faint pale color.

He turned and put both his arms around her, pulling her against his chest. Her small breasts were flattened against him and she could feel the wild rhythm of his heart. She felt the firm length of heat pressed against her lower stomach and bit her lip. He was growing against her, as hard as granite.

"Allison," he murmured, his chest rising and falling with a deep sigh. "Allison, let's . . ." He stopped speaking and took a step away, breaking the spell.

"Ally-oop, let's go!" he cried. He grabbed her hand and broke into a run, dragging her behind.

Nonplussed, she stumbled, then moved her legs as fast as she could to catch up with him. He angled her behind him like a fish fighting a taut line, and they raced in a circle around a hot dog vendor.

"David, stop!" she pleaded, panting and laughing. "I can't keep up!"

"Come on!" He sailed over the crowded streets, his long legs pumping, the tight jeans molding his buttocks and thighs as he moved with the athletic grace of a seasoned runner.

"David, please!"

Then he caught her up in front of the Ripley's Believe It or Not Museum and twirled her in a circle, his head thrown back as he chortled at her shocked peals of girlish laughter. Her eyes shone as the moonlight caught them, her lips parting as she braced herself against his shoulders and begged him to stop.

"David King!"

He obeyed slowly, sliding her down the front of his body. She felt his desire and a sharp answering thrill shot through her, suffusing her veins with golden liquid, settling in her loins.

Though they were laughing, their chests heaving, a tense, erotic yearning steamed beneath the laughter. David's hair was tousled; it ruffled in the wind and she had to restrain herself from combing it back into place, from losing herself in those raven strands . . .

For them the night was silent, save for their panting as they recovered from their run and the unspoken words that passed between their bodies. Both wanted, both needed, both were thinking of the same thing.

"So, onward," David said, and, taking her hand, joined the throngs that jostled down the street.

They bought some crab legs and took turns digging the tasty meat out of them. They bought a cone of cotton candy and giggled like two children as they melted it on the tips of their tongues. After some urging, David chased her through the wax museum, dragging her past the Chamber of Horrors when she decided she was too squeamish to endure it.

They laughed, they window-shopped at the cheesy T-shirt stands and the more rarefied art galleries. Midnight found them in each other's arms, slow dancing on a tiny dance floor at Noonie's, one of David's special places. The regularly scheduled rock band had the night off, and David was glad of it. In its place, a discreet trio played guitar, bass, and sax. The music was languid, restrained, hypnotic.

"You smell so good," David murmured as he pressed his hands over her shoulder blades.

"White Shoulders," she said, struggling not to rest her head against his chest. She was tired from the mad pace David had set, tired of pretending the wild spell of wanting had been permanently broken. David's body was crying out for hers. It was evident in every movement he made, every glance he shot her way. And in the hot firmness of his body she felt his desire. Closing her eyes, she imagined his passion, simmering inside him, waiting.

"You feel so good," he went on.

She said nothing in reply, but she thought, Mister, so do you.

"You're wacked out, aren't you?" he said drowsily, looking down at her. "You've had a long day, Detective Jones."

She nodded. "I don't think I can keep up with you. You move at the speed of light, and I'm a saunterer." She laughed self-consciously. "My idea of a big night is a hot bath and a book."

"A murder mystery, I suppose," he said, smiling.

"But of course. What do you read?"

"Car repair books. Gadget catalogues. Science fiction."

"But of course." She tried to smother a yawn and failed.

"You are tired," he murmured. "Let's go home, my Bathsheba." He toyed with the ringlets at the nape of her neck. "You know, King David's lover? She seduced him by taking a bath in full view of his bedroom window."

"Brazen hussy," Allison said, trying to ignore the huskiness of his voice. What would it be like to bathe with him in the moonlight? Laughing, soaping each other . . .

"Let's go home," David repeated urgently.

The music trickled away. Allison's heart began to thunder. Home? Did he mean her home, his home, to sleep or to . . .?

Saying nothing, they finished the dance and ambled off the floor. David slid her arms into her trench coat and angled her fedora on her head, touching her nose as he nodded his approval. His back muscles worked as he pulled on his own coat, which had been slung over his shoulder most of the evening, and pulled his car keys from his jeans pocket.

Inside the car, David automatically slipped a kinetic rock tape into the player, saw the serene line of Allison's jaw as she rested her head against the seat, and switched off the player before the jarring music had time to blast her. He glanced at her often as he drove back to her house, and saw her lashes sweep downward as she blinked, apparently lost in thought. Once her chest rose and fell in a sigh and she brushed some of her curls away from her forehead.

He walked her to the door without saying a word. When they paused on the threshold, he felt her stiffen, saw the wary look in her eye as she fished for her key.

When he put his hand on her arm, she started. Flushing, she riffled through her purse.

"They're in here somewhere," she muttered.

He gave her forearm a gentle squeeze. "Do you want me to look?"

She gave a nervous laugh, ducking her head so that her fedora hid her face from him. "Good heavens, no! Women never let me go through their purses!"

That wasn't universally true, but he didn't see any advantage in debating the point. As he'd been driving over there, his thought was to seize on any advantage he could to find the Magic Way to her bedroom upstairs. He'd wanted to keep her in this dazed, somnolent state until he was in a better position to rouse her from her semi-slumber.

But the damnedest thing was that now, watching her frantically digging through her purse, blushing and uneasy, he felt his mind changing. Oh, the ardor was still there, the desire, but suddenly, even more than he wanted her in his arms, he wanted her to be comfortable with him.

She lifted her head, an overbright grin on her face. "Here they are," she said lightly. "I swear, I should have them glued to my forehead." Now that was brilliant, she thought. Definitely something Garbo would come up with. A memorable line from a memorable movie called *The Lady Freezes Up*.

David took the key from her. Her lips parted and her blue eyes grew huge as he bent down to the lock. Then he turned the knob and slowly pushed the door open.

The barks and yammers hit him like a blast of frigid air. He smiled his crooked smile and gestured for her to go in.

Before she did so, he kissed her forehead.

"Good night, my lovely," he said. He cocked his head. "Didn't Raymond Chandler write a book with that title?"

She was both relieved and disappointed that he wasn't coming in. Maybe he didn't want to, she thought, shaking her head. But she knew that wasn't the case. She could feel his desire.

"It wasn't 'Good Night,' " she said. "It was 'Farewell.' "

She held her hand out for the key and closed her fingers around it. "I had a lovely time. Good night."

Without another word, she slipped into her house. As he closed the door, David heard the chorus of the canine welcoming committee and Allison's cheerful "Hello, guys. Miss me?"

He stood on the stoop for a moment, listening as she walked into the kitchen. He felt locked out, like a kid refused admittance to a movie that he desperately wanted to see. He remembered when he'd left the auto plant back home in Detroit, pink slip in hand, and how he'd realized the machines were still humming and the men who hadn't been laid off were continuing on without him.

He listened a while longer, trying to imagine what she was doing. He worried that she hadn't locked the door, and then he wondered if he should go on in and do his bachelor thing, sweep her off her feet and into his little black book.

He breathed a sigh of relief when he heard her turn the key in the lock, because she was safe. And unattainable.

Yet, strangely enough, that was all right. If she didn't want to sleep with him just yet, he didn't want to force himself on her. He liked her too much. He respected her and cared for her.

"Oh, Lord," he murmured, "I'm in big, bad trouble. I think I'm falling in love with her."

He rubbed his chin. "Oh, dear Lord, and I've got it bad."

Five

Four days passed without a word from David. Allison spent the first two of them hovering near the phone, feeling more and more foolish—and hurt—as time went on. Obviously he wasn't going to call. He hadn't seen in her whatever he'd hoped to find.

"Darn," she muttered, crouching behind the trash cans at the rear of Christine's Mini-Mart.

"Shh," Barry whispered, "you'll scare him away."

She peered up at her nephew. He was having more fun than Mike Hammer working a case in a massage parlor. Dressed in his full "human fly" regalia of black turtleneck, black corduroy pants, black boots, and a black ski mask—for heaven's sake—he was plastered against the wall above her head, using the fire escape ladder as home base.

It bothered her that she was encouraging his bizarre hobby; as a good aunt, she supposed she should have refused his offer to provide overhead surveillance. After all, she'd been squabbling with her sister all summer over him.

But, as a good detective, she acknowledged the merits of having a bird's-eye view of the scene of the crime. The owner of Christine's, whose name was Tom, was willing to pay a handsome reward for the apprehension of the four-legged thieves who kept raiding his trash cans and leaving debris all over the alley.

There were certain breeds of dogs that ran in packs, and others that scavenged. There were dogs who did both, and those were large and aggressive. So it was nice to have a backup in case the plunderer was as big as a Plott hound. But usually she worked her beat alone.

Alone. Again. She sighed. Oh, well, at least she hadn't had enough time to get attached to David.

Tell me another, Jones, she chided herself. Tell me it doesn't hurt that he told you the truth—he didn't want to get involved.

"Darn."

Barry glared down at her, pulling up his ski mask.

"Aunt Al, be quiet. You keep mumbling to yourself."

"Sorry," she mumbled.

"Hey, I hear something," Barry whispered. "It's coming from the end of the alley."

Sure enough, there it was, the pitter-patter of little feet. Allison's sharp senses went on alert as she crept forward, peering over the lid of a pungent collection of rotting lettuce and lemons and a flyer for Nuke Awareness Day over at UC Berkeley. At the far end of the alley something was nosing around among the cans, panting heavily. It came closer, almost close enough to see, a big black shadow, and then—

A car roared up behind her and Barry, the sound of squealing brakes ricocheting off the graffiti-saturated walls. Allison jumped into the air and Barry swung from the fire escape, both crying out. The dog, a Labrador from her brief glimpse of it, hightailed it out of there, flashing past them.

"Hi," David said, climbing out of a silver Jaguar. "Looking for lunch?"

"Grab him! Don't let him go!" Allison shouted frantically, flailing her arms.

It was too late. David didn't react quickly enough and the Mini-Mart Marauder bounded away.

"You blew my cover!" Allison cried, and then, her

heart catching up with her mind, she flushed and added, "Hi."

The inverted triangle of his shoulder, torso, and hips was splendidly enhanced by a vested navy wool suit. Cuff links flashed as he held out his hands to steady her when she stumbled against a trash can, awkward both in her haste and her relief and joy at seeing him again. He smelled much better than overripe lemons. His sharp, vivid features were more appealing than wilted lettuce. She was more aware of his nuclear energy than all the Berkeley students at twenty Nuke Awareness Days.

"I was just in the neighborhood . . ." he began, and laughed to himself at the poor excuse. *If she believes that, she'll believe anything, King,* he thought. *And Allison Jones is not the gullible type.*

He'd missed her badly and he'd wanted to phone her, going so far as to dial her number and hang up before the first ring. But he didn't want to scare her off by crawling all over her. So he'd waited and waited, until he'd waited too long and couldn't stand it anymore. Unable to reach her at home, he'd left his office and gone searching for her. It was only by pure chance that he'd seen her hovering between the rotting produce and the stack of newspapers for the Kiwanis Club.

Pure chance and four hours of doggedly combing the byways and alleyways of town, that is.

"Sorry I bird-dogged you," he said, trying another tack. "I gather that was somebody's missing pet?"

Before she could reply, Barry flattened himself against the wall of the market and began, without any apparent leverage, to crawl toward the ground. His legs and arms moved in eerie slow-motion, like a sated spider, not like the fly he'd taken as his moniker.

"Hey, Batman, what's up?" David drawled. Barry gave him a short nod.

"It's not Batman, it's the Human Fly of 'Frisco," Allison said, finding her voice at last. His eyes were a warm brown, like strong tea. *Just in the neighborhood,* really? Or just in the neighborhood because he'd been looking for her? At the moment, she didn't care.

"Nobody who lives in San Francisco says 'Frisco,'" David said.

"Yeah?" Barry asked, concerned. "But it goes so well with 'Fly.'"

Inwardly David was trying to regroup. She didn't want to get involved because she was busy all the time, he reminded himself. And he'd just interrupted her work. Bravo. What did he do for an encore?

He scratched his head, unaware that the sight of his long, wedding-ringless fingers sent a sharp thrill through the object of his musings. "Listen, I've got to run, but I was wondering if you'd be free some night this week."

Barry snorted while Allison pretended to mentally consult her busy social calendar. She reminded herself that she should say she *was* busy and let that be the end of it. But she ignored her own advice, just as she ignored Barry's not-so-private amusement at her sham. Teenagers, she noted, had no sense of tact. No discretion. No subtlety.

"As a matter of fact," she said at last, waving her hand in a gesture that made light of the coincidence, "it looks like I'm free tonight."

Barry snorted again. She whirled on him. "Are you catching a cold?" she asked with a rigid expression of concern.

He might be tactless, but he wasn't stupid. "No, Aunt Allison," he murmured. "Just something caught in my throat."

"I told you to stay out of those trash cans," she said, trying to show he was forgiven. Instead, he pulled off his ski mask and frowned indignantly.

"Aunt Al, I didn't do—"

"I think your aunt's just teasing you," David interrupted, amused. "You're free this evening? That's great. So am I." Or would be after a phone call. If he kept canceling blind dates, he was going to get a bad reputation.

Maybe they'd ban him from next year's bachelor book. Bob had arranged this one all the way from the honeymoon suite of the Hukilau Hotel on the Island of Hawaii, promising wedding bells in six weeks if David went through with it.

"And I'll recoup the money I spent for this trip," Bob had added before Patricia batted him with a pillow.

Wedding bells. David shivered. "I'll pick you up at eight," he told Allison, clearing his throat. "Will that be all right?"

"Yes." The little voice inside her brain was screaming "Don't do it! Desist! Resist!" but she shook her head and smiled at David. "That'll be fine."

"I'll see you then." He descended from the clouds and planted a soft kiss on her lips. "And dress up," he added. "We're going first class tonight."

"How nice." Oh, dear. She only had an economy-class wardrobe. Steerage, almost.

"I'm going back downtown," he went on. "I'm sorry I didn't drive a car with room for more than two." He gave Barry a meaningful glance, but it was lost on the boy.

"Too bad," Barry said. "We're going back home, and it takes forever on the bus. We have to change twice."

She was going home. She wasn't busy. Maybe he should lobby for lunch.

But he cast a glance at Allison, whose dainty brows were furrowed and whose dainty thumbnail was being mercilessly chewed, and decided to leave well enough alone.

"It takes us over an hour," Barry went on. He pulled off a pair of black gloves and bent over a toolbox David had missed before. Its contents revealed chains, hooks, pulleys—the esoteric necessities of a human fly.

"Is that so?" David said instead. "Let me fix that." He leaned over the passenger side of the Jag, picked up a phone, and began to dial. "King here," he said. "I need a courtesy limo ASAP." Quickly he gave the address and brief directions.

Barry breathed, "All right," and David shrugged.

"Hey, to me it's nothing. It's my business." He looked at Allison and said, "I'll start sending a car around in the mornings, the way I did last week. Will you promise me you'll use it and stop taking these stupid buses?"

She didn't respond. Locked in a cycle of alternating euphoria and anxiety, she was staring straight ahead and doing mortal damage to her thumbnail. A dress, she thought dispiritedly. Where is Cinderella going to get a dress?

He hunkered down, raising her fedora and squinting at her.

"Yoo-hoo, anybody home?"

She started. "I'm sorry. What were you saying?"

He grinned at her. "I asked you if the car would be all right."

The car? All right? She didn't have the slightest idea what he was talking about. Perhaps he was afraid to park on her block. Heavens, her neighborhood was old, but it wasn't bad.

"It'll be fine," she murmured, too preoccupied to go into it with him now.

There was smething about his face when he smiled, she thought, watching the grin grow across his features. It didn't exactly soften the sharp angles; if anything, it made them more pronounced. With his square chin, aquiline nose, and the straight, high plains of his cheeks, it made him look—what was the right word—

"Awesome!" Barry cried as a two-toned Rolls glided to a stop behind David's Jag. The upper part was a flat silver; the body a sedate soapstone green. Allison came to and gaped at it.

"What's this?"

The chauffeur, dressed in a proper cap and blue tunic, opened his door and spoke to David.

"Good afternoon, Mr. King," he said. "I was in the neighborhood when the call came in."

David chuckled softly. The neighborhood was getting to be a crowded place. "Take them wherever they want to go. But have the lady home by seven fifty-nine."

"Yes, sir." He walked around the car and opened the passenger door with a flourish. "Madam," he invited, standing at attention.

Allison's lips parted. "I didn't . . ." she began, then climbed in, embarrassed about her casual attire and the way Barry was bouncing on the plush seat and crying, "Totally awesome! All right!"

David spoke privately to the man, then poked his head in the window. "Everything satisfactory?"

"Of course," Allison said, "only—"

"Then I'll see you tonight, Detective Jones."

He turned to go, but Allison tugged at his sleeve, her face afire. She felt so gauche, so way out of her league.

"Um." She lowered her voice. "I only have bus fare with me," she said earnestly. "I can't tip him."

He looked hurt. "Allison, I told you I take care of my ladies, didn't I? Don't worry. I've handled it." To ease her obvious discomfort he added, "I promised him my firstborn son."

She smiled, grateful for his suaveness. He could handle anything, she thought admiringly. He was charming.

What do you expect from page thirty-five? the little voice taunted. He's not being thoughtful, he's just being clever. Unlike some folks we both know, Allison. The Fourth of July hasn't even come yet and here you are busily setting yourself up for another disappointment. Ah, vows cheaply made in North Beach were vows easily broken in the back seat of a fancy car.

"Until tonight," David said, touching her hand. Then he walked ahead of the limo and climbed into his Jag.

"Where to, madam?" asked the chauffeur.

"Sausalito!" Barry piped, but Allison shook her head.

"Home, please," she said, and gave him her address.

Allison finished the glass of champagne and peaches and moved back slightly as the waiter appeared at her side and spirited it away.

"That was delicious," she told David, wishing she had

some more sophisticated way of putting it. They had just finished the interlude between course numbers two and three, and her repertoire of compliments had consisted of "That was tasty. Oh, yes, very piquant. Mm, I liked that." And now, "That was delicious." Well, what did one say about champagne and peaches? "That had a delicate bouquet"? Or the ever-popular, "This must be costing you a fortune"?

She was gradually realizing that David King had fortunes to burn. For one thing, he was wearing a tux that fit his marvelous body like a glove. The only person she'd ever known who owned a tuxedo was her father, and he wore it once a year to the Cornucopia Ball put on by the Cornucopia Corporation, the wholesale grocery conglomerate that employed him as a shipping supervisor. He had owned that tux for twenty-nine years. David's looked stylish and new.

She licked her lips. The last time she'd gone out with a guy wearing a tuxedo was to her senior prom. Her next-door neighbor, Elwood, had been forced by his mother to take her, and he'd spent the whole night regaling her with interesting facts about data processing. Allison had not been suave enough to hide her boredom. Elwood now owned a huge computer corporation which was in the process of going public. Allison's mother liked to mention it occasionally when she called.

During her reminisces about "Tuxedos I Have Known and Dated," David leaned forward, and murmured, "You look delicious, too, Allison. In fact, you're the cat's meow."

She smiled, shifting in her chair. A mauve-beaded chemise hung to her knees, and, beneath it, a cream-and-mauve silk skirt molded her ankles while she searched under the table for her shoes. Mrs. Scarpare, who had once been a singer on the hotel concert circuit in the thirties, had offered to lend Allison the gown, going so far as to alter it to fit her. She'd also lent her the matching silk shoes, which, unfortunately, were a size too small, but necessary, as Allison had nothing else that came close to the magnificence of the ensemble. The first chance she'd had, she had eased them off and hidden them within the folds of her gown.

For this beneficence, Mr. Scarpare had demanded to know the name of the horse she was betting on, apparently unable to believe that things like daily limousine service could be acquired in any other way. After Mrs. Scarpare had appealed to her to humor him, she'd finally thrown her hands in the air and said "King."

"Thanks for the flowers," she murmured, touching her hair. A spray of white orchids, delivered at seven-thirty in a chauffeured Bentley, nestled in her jet curls, which were swept up Grecian style and held in place with a white silk ribbon. Ringlets and tendrils cascaded where they would, grazing her temples and her long neck. She also wore a silver choker that had belonged to Aunt Mildred; inside the oval locket was a sepia print of Uncle Arthur.

Beneath the table, David's fingers fidgeted with his cuff links. He'd thought to wine and dine her, resuming Plan A—Operation Riveter—by bringing her to the Carnelian Room, high atop the Bank of America building. He'd made sure they'd gotten the best table, the one in the corner near the pointed windows, so Allison could see both the Bay Bridge and the Golden Gate. In the glossy black night they looked like strings of Christmas tree lights, looped and shining and beautiful. He'd planned everything and he'd failed somewhere.

Because Allison seemed about as thrilled as a little girl who's discovered a gift certificate to a hardware store inside her Christmas stocking.

She was boring him, Allison thought dismally, searching for her shoes. He was spending all this money and he was over there frowning. Oh, she could just die.

It wasn't until she blinked that she realized she'd been staring at him. Flushing, she looked down and saw that a plate decorated with bits of beef and beautiful, ornate puffs of potatoes had been snuck in between the rows of silverware without her noticing.

"Penny for your thoughts," David said. He took her hand in his and ran his upper lip over her nails. "You're so quiet tonight."

She hesitated for a moment, not wanting to hurt his feelings, but not sure she could hide hers much longer. He tilted his head and the light danced in his eyes. Behind him the panorama of bridges and stars glowed, and Allison wished she could just relax and savor the fruits of David's triumphant battle with life.

"Is there something wrong?" David pressed. "Please, Ally-oop, tell me."

The "Ally-oop" did it. It was as if he were saying, "Hey, it's just me, David. Remember? The guy at the Hubba?"

Then she looked down at his hand holding hers, at the elegant monogram ring. They really had nothing in common, she thought sadly. Even if she were looking for a boyfriend—which she wasn't—it couldn't be David. She didn't fit in with his lifestyle at all.

"Hey," he whispered, "am I keeping you awake?"

He had the longest lashes and the darkest eyes. The most compelling smile . . .

"If you must know," she said, taking a deep breath, "I'm floundering, I'm out of my element. My shoes are too small." She blinked. How had that slipped out?

His lips curved up in a most appealing way and he turned her hand over, straightening out her fingers as he stroked the center of her palm. "You're not out of your element, Allison. You're the most elegant woman here."

In a borrowed dress, she almost said, but didn't. Instead she picked up her fork and began to eat while David continued to stroke her other hand. She tried to ignore the way it throbbed and tingled.

"I'm sorry your shoes are too small," he added. "I know that can take the edge off your appetite." One side of his mouth twisted into a wry grin. "But you're covering it nicely."

Her eyes were china-blue, clear as water. "David, I like you," she began.

Uh-oh, he thought, she always followed that up with bad news.

"But I really don't think I'm—"

"Shush and eat your food," he interrupted, wrapping her hand around his, securing her fingers like the clasp on a bracelet on the pulse of his vein. It was beating rapidly. Perhaps he wasn't bored after all.

"But, David—"

He let go of her hand and watched it disappear into her lap. She's floundering, he repeated to himself. Of course. How insensitive could a guy get? With her income, she probably dined out at McDonald's. She was so fiercely independent that it was probably driving her crazy, not knowing how much this meal cost. He smiled inwardly. Perhaps it was better that she didn't know. The price of the wine alone would have kept her animals in Tender Vittles for a month. Make that three.

And she had found the courage to confess that to him—in a roundabout way. Allison Jones, you're a gorgeous puzzle, he said silently. Able to hold your own in a dive like the Hubba, as regal as a duchess in one of the plushest rooms in town, and yet you have an artlessness that makes me want to protect you and pamper you like a sheltered Victorian lady.

He put his fork down, folded his hands together and leaned his chin on them. "Ya wanna blow dis joint?" he asked quietly.

Allison looked up, startled. Her mouth was full, but her eyes spoke for her, saying more than she would have liked him to know.

He called the waiter over and murmured to him. The waiter murmured back in a grave, accommodating voice. Meanwhile, Allison swallowed and tried to intervene. She knew David had selected everything in advance, and paid for it, too, and she couldn't stand the idea of all that food and money going to waste just because she had the Orphan Ally jitters.

But the man tiptoed away and David touched his napkin to his lips in a conclusive way.

"David, we don't have to go," she said. "I mean, I'd like to stay. Goodness, I haven't eaten much and I'm starved . . ."

"Allison, you're the world's worst liar," David said jovially. "Come on, tell me the truth. Do you really want to sit here for two more hours?"

"I'm having a lovely time, really," she insisted.

"I'm not."

She twisted her fingers in her lap. "I know," she said, guilt shading her tone so that the words came out as an apology. "I guess I'm not classy eno—"

David rose. The waiter glided behind Allison's chair and the captain appeared and presented her with a single long-stemmed rose, saying, "Mit ze compliments of ze Carnelian Room. I hope you will come again, *gnägide Fraulein*."

David touched the small of her back as he guided her out of the room. "Thank you, Gunther. She will," he said simply.

They were the only ones in the elevator as it zoomed down to the bottom of the building. Allison touched the rose to her chin, inhaling the sweet fragrance.

David moved behind her and put his hands on her shoulders, leaning over her. His chest was pressed against her back and she straightened, but his hands prevented her from putting more than an inch of distance between their bodies. She could feel the heat of his flesh through her clothes, the whisper of his breath against her temple. His fingers were dark against the pastel gown, the nails white and trimmed. Is there any part of him that doesn't drive me crazy? she thought, wishing she'd left her detective's keen senses at home.

"Feeling better?" he asked, sliding his hands from her shoulders to her upper arms, his thumbs making little circles on her bare skin.

"I hope I didn't embarrass you," she said, her lids flickering against the tide of sensation he was eliciting. "I feel a little foolish now, bolting like that."

"Then don't bolt next time," he replied. "Like now."

He turned her around and kissed her, splaying one hand against her shoulder blades, the other melding into the small of her back. He tasted of wine as he stole past her defenses and invaded her mouth, nearly crushing her in his embrace as he drank deeply of her. Her breasts were flattened against his chest, the nipples painful buds of a sudden, sharp yearning that hit her like lightning.

"Oh, Allison," he said, undulating his hips in a slow Gypsy dance of smoky desire. "You're the most desirable woman I've ever met. I can't keep my hands off you, even for a moment. Let's stop the elevator and—"

Too late. The doors opened at the lobby floor to reveal a middle-aged man and woman, formally dressed, gaping at him and Allison.

David winked at the old man as he grabbed Allison's rose and clenched it between his teeth. "Olé," he said, and ushered Allison out of the elevator.

He was driving a stately, cream-colored Jaguar limo that night, and as the valet rolled it to a stop in front of them, David kissed Allison's cheek. "Don't worry," he said, opening the door and helping her in. "We'll soon have those shoes off."

She jerked her head up. "What?"

He slid in behind the wheel. "Where we're going," he went on, undoing his tux tie, "you won't need them."

She narrowed her eyes at him. "And just where are we going?"

He shrugged. "It's a surprise."

He was right. It was a surprise. Allison could only imagine that he was making his bachelor move to get her into bed, and braced herself for a confrontation. But when he turned the car into the line for the Spruce Four Drive-In, her mouth dropped open. The Spruce Four was having "Bogartmania Nights." Tonight they were showing *Casablanca* and *The Maltese Falcon*.

"Oh, this is terrific!" Allison cried as David angled into a space and set the parking brake of the stunning car. People were gawking at them, opening their Chevy and

Datsun doors and gesturing to each other. Kids paraded past and hovered in groups, pointing and discussing the mysterious stranger in their midst.

"It *is* Amy Irving!" Allison heard a young girl squeal.

David seemed not to notice. He was busily positioning the speaker box in the window behind his seat. That accomplished, he glanced at her and said, "Let's move to the backseat. We'll be more comfortable there."

She thought of protesting, but saw that he had a point. The steering wheel was close to his chest and his head was brushing the ceiling.

They moved. Then David folded the front seats forward, giving the two of them plenty of room to lounge, and undid the top two studs of his shirt. Putting them into his pocket, he settled his arm on the seat back above Allison's neck and said, "I should've brought you here instead of the Carnelian Room. I planned it for later."

Aware of his arm above her head, she eased off her shoes. "After a four-hour dinner? Don't you ever get tired?"

He winked at her. "Not of having fun with a beautiful woman, Bathsheba."

"Oh, you're the Goliath of flatterers."

"Will flattery get me somewhere?"

She said nothing, only swallowed and adjusted the folds of her dress. But her heart was thundering and she felt his heat like hands on her skin. Her body began to respond. Her stomach contracted and her nipples pressed against the delicate lace bra that barely contained her breasts.

They sat in silence. Allison listened to the increasing rhythm of her heart throughout the cartoon and the previews, acutely aware that David had done nothing to cause it except sit beside her in the dark intimacy of the car. She was tensing all over, her senses heightened. She felt the cool, smooth leather beneath her back and bottom, smelled its mellowed patina of age. The satin of her gown rustled as she shifted, caressing her, sending chills through her as she imagined the layers of beautiful fabric being lifted away . . .

She pressed her legs together and closed her eyes when she heard David chuckle at something on the screen. She opened them, to see the French policeman at Rick's Place, and was shocked to find she'd been oblivious to the unfolding of the movie. She hadn't even realized that it had started.

Her pulse was racing. David moved and his arm brushed the back of her head. She breathed in slowly. Her breasts and lips were tingling; the secret place between her legs was beginning to pulsate.

He couldn't stand this any longer, David thought, watching her out of the corner of his eye. If ever a woman wanted a man, she wanted him.

At that moment Allison looked at him, eyes as large as cerulean moons. Her lips were moist, parted, as if she were going to speak.

But she didn't say a word. She only looked at him, perhaps not knowing that her expression was one of pleading and invitation. Of need. Of desire.

"Allison," he murmured, and all at once he was raining shimmering kisses on her forehead and cheeks, burying his face in the scent of orchids before he found the perfect petals of her lips. They were soft, yielding, and she gasped when he eased them apart and entered her mouth, the hot length of his tongue stroking the tip of hers. He claimed possession of her, arms bruising her against his chest as his lips branded hers, his tongue searing her with a foretoken of what was to come.

"David—" she managed before he kissed her again. His fingers shook as they found the beaded straps of her chemise and eased them over her shoulders. He kissed the bare flesh, moaning deep in his throat, molding her delicate collarbones with his hot, pliant lips.

She closed her eyes and allowed her head to fall into the cradle of his palm, feeling the silky curls of her hair spilling across her cheeks and forehead. Like butterfly wings, his fingers fluttered down the arch of her neck, weaving in and out of her hair, bringing a lock of it to his lips.

"Your hair's so soft," he said, laying it back over her ear and stroking it. "I love to touch it."

His hands dropped lower, tracing the décolletage of her dress. Her breasts were almost completely exposed, the bodice of the gown held up only by the way Allison pressed her arms against her sides, which accentuated her cleavage. David's fingers roamed over the pale mounds, darting underneath the mauve satin in search of the growing peaks of her nipples.

"Allison, I want you," he whispered, nibbling her neck just below her ear. "I want this."

Her head jerked up as he cupped her between the legs, pressing his hand over her femininity. It responded at once to his bold assault, and Allison struggled to contain her reaction.

"No, David," she said hoarsely, trying to grab his thick wrist. "Not here. Not now."

But he ignored her, his hand sliding down her leg to the hem of her skirt. His fingers dove beneath it and retraced the fiery route, delineating each rigid muscle of her calf and inner thigh as he sought the treasure of her womanhood.

He looked down at her, at her heaving breasts. Bending his head, he urged the bodice farther down, revealing her strapless bra.

His eyes flared; she saw them through half-closed lids as she writhed within his grasp. She should stop him, she should. She couldn't let him do this.

But the urgency, the unexpected ferocity of his advance, had completely overpowered her. She had expected a pass, maybe an attempt or two at a kiss. But this . . .

His hand paused at the top of her stocking and he caught his breath. He had discovered she was wearing a garter belt.

"Allison," he said softly. "Beautiful, sexy Allison.

Dressed like a vamp and trembling like a virgin. You're a sultry paradox, my love."

"Please," she gasped, unaware that she'd spoken. "You don't know what you're doing to me."

His laugh was low and husky. "Of course I do. But I don't think *you* know what you're doing to *me*."

"I'm not doing . . . anything," she managed to say.

"Oh, yes you are."

He picked up one of her hands and pressed it against himself. He was full of wanting, hot, hard. She felt herself opening up inside, blossoming like a flower, the primitive call to surrender driving her to spread her thighs apart the least little bit.

His hand moved upward, fingers grazing the edge of her panties. Her muscles contracted violently, lifting her bottom off the seat. David's lips sucked at her nipples through the bra, each in turn, making her whimper and moan as he supported her buttocks with his other hand.

Then he grazed the silky strands of hair that twined like gossamer flower stems along the outer portals of her womanhood, holding Allison in thrall. He watched her, thrilling to her passion.

"Oh, David, stop!" she cried, but he forced her to accept his intimate touch. A flush of scarlet flared up her chest and over her throat as she fought against the sheer pleasure, knowing it was wrong, that she shouldn't, knowing that she didn't have the willpower to stop him.

"Take the pleasure I offer you," he demanded, holding her as she sought to move away. "Don't fight it, my sweet."

"I'm . . . afraid," she blurted out, lifting her head. But he pushed her back with another kiss, and another, and another. Her resistance ebbed. Her shoulders sagged, then arched as David did marvelous things to her femininity.

"Don't be," he whispered. "I won't hurt you. I'd never hurt you, ever."

"But . . ." she began, and her voice trailed off. Words and thoughts were slipping away from her, dissolving into ripples that skittered down her spine. Instead of pushing David away, she clung to him, unaware that she was doing so. Her body had completely conquered her mind.

Then Allison began to pant, the chant of eons that told him she was near the crest. So soon, he thought wonderingly. He had only guessed at the fire beneath her cool exterior. Dear heaven, how he wanted it to consume him.

"David, we've got to stop," she groaned, coming back to herself. She grimaced, her body heaving, her breasts swelling against her bra. "This is a public place. Please, stop."

"The windows are steamed up," he whispered in her ear. "No one can see."

"I'm—" She inhaled sharply. "No involve—"

"Just let go," David commanded her softly. "Let go and pretend I'm inside you. "

The last vestiges of rational thought were shocked at what she was doing, at what they were both doing. But the rest of her—the woman in her—was straining, reaching, struggling. Her body writhed. She was fierce and wild, like a savage animal in a frenzy of motion and power. Heat was building up inside her, and exquisite delight, and more, and more, and . . .

"David!" she cried, and she exploded into a million points of light, shimmering and scintillating as they rushed apart and crashed into a galaxy of suns. She was nothing and everything; she was freer than she had ever been; she was exquisite release and David's creature of blind passion.

David. She opened her eyes, surprised to find her cheeks were wet.

He peered up at her through his abundant lashes and smiled. "Wow," he murmured.

Swallowing, she said nothing, only tried to cover herself as she sat up.

"We shouldn't have done that," she managed to say, averting her eyes as he helped her pull up her dress.

"Why not?" His voice as casual, but inside he was shaking. *I love you, I love you,* he was shouting. *I love you and I want you to love me back, and, by God, I'll do or say whatever it takes to accomplish it.*

She touched the locket at her throat. She was so embarrassed that she wanted to shrink into one of the ridges in the upholstery. She'd never let go like that in her entire life. And with a man she barely knew.

"Why not?" he repeated.

"I already told you," she said. "I don't want to get involved."

Damn, damn, damn, David thought. Bob would be howling if he could see me right now. How's it feel when the shoe is on *your* foot, King?

Flashing her a jaunty smile, he said, "Hey, no problem. So who says we're involved?"

She wanted to hit him. She wanted to burst into tears. Instead, she smoothed her rumpled skirt and smiled back. "Just checking," she lied.

And just dying inside.

Six

"That's the dumbest thing you've ever done, Ally-cat," Janet admonished as Allison bet a can of hearts and kidneys on what was, after all, a terrible poker hand.

"No, it's not," Allison replied, sighing. "I've done something much dumber." Very recently.

The group was sitting around Allison's dining room table. The room had been cleared of kittens and other small, furry interruptions, as it always was for poker nights.

Privately, Allison wished for an interruption of another kind—the shrill ring of the telephone. But nothing disturbed the smooth flow of betting as the others placed their final wagers.

"Three of a kind," Janet's beloved Hunter announced, laying down the winning hand. He was a good-looking man with caramel-colored hair and eyes and a cute little mustache that caught the foam in his beer. He had a nice steady job at a brokerage house, and he was as stable as the Rock of Gibraltar—a nicely shaped hunk of ballast for Janet, who tended toward continental drift. She floated from one occupation to another—street mime, artist, rock band singer—and she needed someone like Hunter in her life. And, happily, Hunter needed her.

Allison watched Janet kiss Hunter's cheek, her

friend's eyes glowing with love. Sighing wistfully, she toyed with the sleeves on her scarlet Chinese blouse. It was tucked into pleated black satin slacks—an original she'd found in Aunt Mildred's closet, and one of her favorite outfits. Dangling jade earrings completed her look, and Janet had insisted on making up her eyes, drawing them into an almond shape with smudges of peacock shadow.

How come that never happens to me? Allison wondered, watching Hunter's affectionate response to Janet's kiss. How come men always leave me?

"You're not playing well tonight," said Emma, otherwise known as the Bionic Woman, shuffling the cards two seats over. Her gray hair was the exact shade of her Persian cat's, whom Allison had rescued from a dog pack two years before. "Is there something bothering you, dear?"

"No," she lied. But it had been two days since the drive-in, and David hadn't called.

The doorbell rang. Pausing, Allison counted heads at the table: Emma, Tim, Curt, and the lovebirds. Everybody she'd invited was here. So who could that be?

"Maybe it's your chauffeur wanting to use the bathroom," the Bionic Woman said.

"He only works days, my deah," Janet drawled through her nose. "Milady has to phone for a driver in the evenings."

"Well, la-di-da." Emma fluttered her lashes and everyone chuckled.

"It's probably just the Queen of England." Tim, an airline pilot for whom Allison had also once rescued a cat, waved the deck of cards. "But tell her to get her butt in here so we can play some real poker. I'm ready for action."

Allison nodded vaguely, hurrying to the door. He'd call first, she told herself, feeling ridiculous for the way her pulse had begun to accelerate. It's not David, so calm down. You're acting like a teenager. You're being stupid. Calm down.

"Good evening," David said as she opened the door. He was lounging against the jamb in an all-white suit, its crisp starkness setting off his black hair and dark eyes. His tie was beige and gray, and he wore a white rose in his lapel. Clean-shaven, smelling faintly of musk, he stood before her like William Powell, urbane and sophisticated and wolfish.

He leaned down and kissed her tenderly, cupping the side of her jaw with his large hand as his lips pressed against hers. She held her breath. A gunpowder trail of pleasure flashed up her spine, ignited by both his presence and the memories of what had passed between them such a short—and long—time ago. Her hands balled into fists, then relaxed, and she knew she was in danger of swooning against his hard chest and dissolving into a pool at his feet.

"I'm sorry I'm late," he said, reluctantly ending the kiss. "Barry told me it'd be okay if I didn't make it exactly on time."

Barry. He must have forgotten to tell her David had called. And that he'd invited him. Now there was a boy with his head in the clouds . . .

Frowning, David tilted his head. "Well, it is okay, isn't it? I hope you're not angry. I had that dumb benefit to go to."

He was speaking as if she knew all about it. Fighting the impulse to touch her hand to her lips to quell the tingling, she stepped back and let him in.

"Of course not," she managed to say. "I'm just glad you could make it."

"I brought some wine." He held out a bottle of burgundy, its cork held in place with a wire cap. "It's a friend's label. Pretty dry."

"Thanks," she murmured, but inside she was asking, When did you call? How many times? Won't you leave now because I'm too happy to see you and I see disaster on my horizon?

"Hey, Allison, who is it?" someone bellowed from the dining room.

"Fresh blood," she heard Tim say.

She paused on the threshold for a moment, her gaze entwining with David's. "Come meet my friends," she said. "I hope you like them."

He laced his fingers through hers and swung her arm. "If they're yours, Ally-oop, I'm sure I will."

They walked together into the room. Janet leaped up from Hunter's lap and clapped her hands.

"David Davidovitch! How great!" She turned to the group. "Look, everybody! It's Allison's new boyfriend!"

Deep purple crept up Allison's neck. "Janet," she said in a low voice, "David's just a fr—"

"Hi, Janet," David cut in smoothly. "How's tricks?"

Janet grinned at him. "Just great. But let me introduce you. This is the Bionic Woman, and Captain Curt, and Captain America, and this is my Hunter."

Emma bobbed her head at him. "I'm also known as Emma Wabash."

"She has a pacemaker," Janet explained. "And Captain Curt is a radio talk-show host."

Curt half-stood and held out his hand, mumbling, "How d' you do?" He wore an U.S. Festival visor that hid his eyes, but the rest of his face was dour. Talking, apparently, was his profession, not his hobby.

"And I'm Captain America, I suppose," Tim said, shuffling the cards. "I work for TWA. Allison saved my cat once."

"Flying Tiger was stuck in a tree in Golden Gate Park," Janet explained, "and Allison climbed up to get him. Tim's afraid of heights."

David regarded the pilot. "Doesn't that make your job, ah, difficult?"

Tim flushed. "I'm seeing someone about it."

"He can't get it up past twenty thousand feet," Janet chirruped. "The plane, I mean. Oh, look, you brought wine! We only have beer and Coke."

"Have a seat, David." Emma indicated the empty chair beside hers and looked around him to smile at Allison. "We're playing Communist Dog Pound tonight."

Tim chuckled at David's confused expression. "Allison provides the chips," he explained. He held up a dog biscuit. "We just divide them up at the beginning of the game and play until someone has them all. Then we give them back to her."

"We call her The State," Emma chimed in. Her face was rosy as she looked at David, her eyes shiny and appreciative. She threw another glance of approval at Allison, who pretended not to notice.

"I have tons of dog treats," Allison added. "They make great bribes for my stoolies on the streets."

David laughed, accepting a beer from Captain America after slipping off his jacket and rolling up his shirt sleeves. Allison watched the muscles shift under his tanned skin as he raised his mug to his lips and took a healthy swallow.

"Well, deal me in," David said. "I'll try anything once."

Including falling in love? an insidious little voice whispered as Allison took her seat beside him.

She held up some multicolored treats. "Blues are ones, reds are fives, and greens are tens." She picked up a bone-shaped biscuit. "Fifties." A can of food. "Hundreds." And the *pièce de résistance*, a purple squeeze toy mouse: "Thousands."

"Thousands?" David asked, amused. "How do I keep from breaking the bank—or The State, as it were?"

"Easy," she said, her light tone belying the tumult inside her. "We shoot you."

"Communist poker," Emma reminded him.

"Then The State should wither away," David drawled, drawing a line down Allison's arm.

She saw Janet and Emma exchange pleased, amused looks, and set her jaw as she began to count out David's stake, straining to keep her hands from shaking. "Everybody starts out with the same amount," she said to break the silence.

" 'From each according to his ability . . .' " David said.

" 'To each according to his need,' " Allison finished blithely.

She paled as David fixed her with a look, inclining his head. Though the people around them began to talk among themselves, she heard nothing but David's murmured, "And I need you, Allison. I want you."

Then he examined his pile of doggie delights and scratched his chin. "This is going to take all night," he said.

But it didn't. A few beers later he had enough Milk Bones and Alpo to open his own pet shop. Janet had regaled him with bizarre stories of her life as a street mime; Allison had blushed and stumbled her way through some bad bets; and Captain Curt had spoken a total of five words.

It was fun. These people were zany, and he marveled at how a collection of such diverse personalities could get along so well. Because they all knew Allison, he decided. Because they loved her and wanted to be with her. She was the equalizing factor.

"That's it. I give up," Janet announced as David turned over another straight. She kissed Hunter's cheek. "Come on, baby. We've both got long days tomorrow."

Hunter frowned. "It's only a quarter to ten. We never leave before mid—"

"Hunter," she interrupted, speaking between clenched teeth. She jabbed her head in Allison's direction. "Let's go home."

Allison closed her eyes, only to open them and find David's speculative gaze on her. Beside him, Emma was gathering up her purse, her lips twitching with smug contentment. On the other side of the table, Captain Curt shrugged, laid down his cards, and stood.

"Guess you win," he mumbled. That raised his total to eight words.

"I'll get you next time," Tim offered, stretching. "I guess it is late. I'm flying to New York tomorrow."

"Poor thing," Janet said.

"Cruising at *thirty* thousand," he retorted.

"Maybe you'll see my nephew crawling up the Empire

State Building." Allison tapped her cards. "I shouldn't have bet two cans on three fours, I guess."

"Your mind wasn't on the game at all," Emma agreed. "You must be *very preoccupied*." Another look. Allison sighed.

"Well, Dave, you won fair and square." Hunter shook David's hand and led the way to the front door, draping his arm over Janet's shoulders. The rest of Allison's guests trooped en masse behind him, practically running across the threshold. The door shut with a resounding thud less than two minutes after Janet had cued everyone in to the fact that it was time to leave the young lovers alone.

For which she would either kill her or love her, Allison decided, depending on how the rest of the evening turned out.

She turned to David and ran a hand through her hair. "Not too subtle, are they?" she said, laughing weakly.

"You're beautiful tonight," David murmured. "There's something about you. A radiance."

"Janet spruced me up," she replied, hurrying to the table. "She just joined the Face of the Month Club. Makeup, I mean."

She began to clear off the empty beer mugs and carrot sticks, feeling the air waft around her as he came up behind her.

"Allison," he said, putting his arms around her waist. "Don't do that now."

She stopped moving, forcing herself to breathe as his touch mesmerized her. "All right," she said.

She was nervous, he thought. She was like a skittish fawn. But dammit, she wanted him. And she was going to get him.

"Let's play," he said, and smiled to himself when he felt her stiffen. "Cards." He ran his hands up her back and massaged her tight shoulders. "I'll give you a chance to win it all back from me. Though I don't know about you, Detective Jones. I think you're kind of rusty in the gambling department."

If he only knew, she thought.

"Come on, I dare you," he taunted, expert hands kneading away her hesitation.

She licked her lips. Her throat had gone dry and she wasn't sure if she'd be able to speak. "I'm usually pretty good," she said, lids fluttering as his hands moved across her back. Her entire body was springing to life, each nerve awakened by the electric rhythm of the strokes. It was all she could do to keep from turning around into his embrace.

"I'll bet you are." He pressed himself against her back and kissed the flesh behind her ear. Then he drew out her chair for her and sat in the seat opposite her. "Let's raise the ante," he suggested, patting the table with his palms. "Two blues and a biscuit."

She made a show of considering it, both grateful and disappointed that the massage was over. "I don't know if I'm up to that."

"I'm up," he drawled, leaning forward and taking her hand. He cradled it between both of his, turning it over and kissing her open palm. "Come on, Allison. Let's get down to business here. I'm in the mood for . . . winning."

The moon was peering through the window, hanging over his shoulder. How could he be so handsome and rich, and be sitting here with her? she wondered. How come he kept coming around just when she'd given up?

How long would it be until he went away for good?

She shook her head to clear away the unhappy question. "All right," she said, squaring her shoulders. "I'll deal."

"Let's turn the lights down first." He reached around to the wall behind his chair and flicked a switch, dimming the chandelier above them. The gauzy glow cast a halo of blue into his hair and shaded his eyes below his thick brows.

"That's better," he murmured, studying her for a moment as she dealt the hand. "You were made for muted lights, Allison. Life in soft focus."

"Do you want any cards?" she asked, clearing her throat.

He shook his head. "I'm content. For now."

They placed their bets.

"Call," David said. "What've you got?"

"Two fives," she said dispiritedly, preparing to shove the pot at him.

He held up his hand. "Two threes. You win. I lose."

"Oh." She was surprised. "I didn't expect that," she said, flashing him a triumphant smile. "My luck must be changing."

"Mine too." He stopped her from scooping up her winnings. "I'm changing the rules," he informed her. There was a curious half-smile on his lips as he spoke, a slight tension in his shoulders.

"What?"

Saying nothing, he began to unbutton his vest. Slowly, deliberately, his eyes upon her, he slipped it off and dropped it on the table.

"What are you doing?" she asked, drawing back.

"I told you. Changing the rules. Here, have some more beer."

He poured her a glass from a bottle on the table, then clinked mugs with her and drank. He peered at her through his long lashes, his broad chest moving as he gathered up the discards and put them in a pile near the deck.

He lost again, Slowly his hands worked the buttons of his shirt, and he held Allison captive with his eyes as he drew it open, revealing a clinging, spaghetti-strap T-shirt that outlined firm pectorals and the undulations of his rib cage. His biceps were large and round, his skin the color of cinnamon. The sight of him took her breath away.

"Strip poker," he said. "Your deal again, Allison."

"Now just a minute," she protested, her eyes riveted to his chest. "You said . . . we can't do this!"

"Why not?"

"Because I, well . . . what if Barry walks in?"

"Come on, Allison. You know perfectly well he's spending the night at his friend's house."

"He didn't tell me that!" she cried, throwing down the cards and crossing her arms. "And if you think I'm going to sit here and—and—"

"And anyway, I know he has his own entrance to the attic. Even if he decides to come home, we won't be disturbed."

She had no reply. A triumphant smile spread across David's face as he hooked his fingers underneath the T-shirt straps. He didn't take his eyes off her as he shimmied the clinging fabric over his head.

The moon glowed on his body, losing itself in the shadows and valleys of his chest and stomach. A mat of hair ran down his sculpted torso, swirling around tiny male nipples and into his trousers. As Allison followed its path, she saw his hands move to his belt.

"No," she whispered.

The buckle glinted in the light as David unclasped it. He began to unzip his pants with languid movements that teased and tantalized her. "Yes," he said. "For us, tonight, it's yes."

It would be a simple thing to rise from the chair and leave the room. There was no reason on earth to let him do this, to sit here and watch him take off his clothes in a slow, seductive striptease that had her reeling. The same sense of powerlessness that had overcome her in the drive-in took hold of her now, and she felt as though someone else were controlling her actions, enslaving her will.

And that someone else stood before her now, easing off his pants and underwear, unveiling the splendor of his masculine form. His hips were narrow, his lower belly tight with muscles and deep indentations on either side of his pelvis. His body was a thing of glory, and it wanted her. David stood naked, his desire proudly evident. Tall and imperious, he came toward her.

"David," she whispered, clutching her hands in her lap. Her eyes glittered and widened, betraying the emotion and desire that was churning inside her. She swallowed, feeling his warmth as he neared, breathing in the musky odor of maleness that permeated the space between them.

"I can't wait to undress you, love," he said, picking up her hands and flattening them on his stomach.

His flesh was hot. She drew back, startled, but David eased her to a standing position and held her against the wanting, virile length of his body. His manhood thrust against her lower abdomen, seeking, demanding.

"I want you, Allison," he whispered. "And you want me."

"David . . ." Her voice trailed off, the heat from his skin burning her fingertips. His heart was hammering; she could feel the blood rushing downward into his manhood, preparing for the frenzied moment when all his strength and ardor would be mustered. His chest filled, then emptied, his nipples growing into peaks as he looked down at her. He was not speaking, not touching, merely soaking up the sensations of her hands on his body.

"See how I desire you," he said. "See my body reacting to you. Allison, it's time for us."

Taking her hands in his, he slipped to his knees and pressed his face against the clothed heat of her femininity. She gasped, her head falling back, her hands weaving through his luxurious hair. He was silk and stone, contrary perfection, a puzzle of delight.

His hands cupped her buttocks as he inhaled. "You smell like roses," he murmured. "You're such a dainty, precious thing, Allison."

He moved his hands behind her thighs and lifted her into the air. "Allison, he whispered, "my beauty."

"Oh," she murmured, and the word began a sigh as he drew her down his chest. She held onto his shoulders to balance herself, feeling the working of his muscles, the vitality of his youth and health. Her breasts flattened against his bare chest, the Chinese silk caressing them.

His maleness probed between her legs and her thighs, and her buttocks contracted in response. Wildly, she shook her head.

"No, David," she said, "put me down."

Saying nothing, he shifted her so that one arm supported her back and the other scooped up her legs. Then he kissed her once, tenderly, and headed for the stairway.

"Stop, no," she gasped. "I don't want to go to bed with you."

His look expressed his disbelief. He took the stairs quickly, impatiently, and he didn't wait for her to tell him which room was her bedroom. He simply began to open doors.

"Not that one!" she blurted out. Eyes flashing, he turned the crystal knob. "That's where I'm keeping the animals tonight," she went on. As if to verify her claim, a series of mews and yaps burgeoned on the other side.

He released the knob as if it were electrified. "That leaves door number three," he said, turning around. "And I have the grand prize in my arms."

"David," she began, but he silenced her with a kiss as he carried her into her bedroom.

The lights were off, but the drapes were open, billowing in the night air. The mauves and pale grays of the satin bedspread were washed with moonlight, caught in the brass waves of the headboard. Rainbows from the crystal chandelier above the bed glowed on his shoulders as he gently laid her down, touching a finger to her lips when she parted them in protest. Her ebony hair fanned over the satin pillow like a crown of ravens' wings; her eyes shone like rare jewels. She was so beautiful that he had to close his eyes for a moment before he could speak.

"Allison, I promised you I wouldn't complicate your life," he said. "And I won't. We're each free to do our own thing. But you can't deny what's between us. Every time we touch each other, it's like a living force that grows. I don't know if I understand it, but I'm sure as hell not going to ignore it. Let me make love to you, Allison. I won't force myself on you, though God knows I'm at the point where it's difficult not to. But I'm asking you to let me love you."

He lay down beside her, his weight dipping the bed. Clasping the sides of her chin with his fingers, he turned her face toward his and searched her features. She could feel his maleness push against her hip and a ripple of longing coursed through her. She wanted to touch him, to wrap her hands around his smooth, rigid masculinity, to run her fingers along his tight buttocks and thighs.

"David, I . . ." she began. She wanted to tell him she was afraid. Because she cared for him so much already, and she shouldn't. She barely knew him, and already she was dreading the day he'd leave her. And he would. They all did. She didn't know why, and she was helpless to prevent it. If she made love to him . . .

Helpless. She knew it. She knew she wasn't going to send him away. She couldn't. Her body was reaching for his, yearning for the fulfillment that had taken life back at the Club Hubba Hubba. It was inevitable. She should accept it instead of resisting it. But there was so much fear intermingled with the wanting.

"I'll make you happy," David murmured, caressing her face. His hand trailed down the row of black satin frogs, then cupped her right breast as he covered her lips and cheeks with kisses. Her nipple hardened like a berry and he fondled it between his thumb and forefinger, catching his breath when Allison moaned.

"Little Allison, I'll make you glad you let me love you."

Love you. The words caught at her like tree branches, urging her to stop him. This wasn't love to him. This was an expression of their mutual desire, but nothing more. Doing this could only lead to heartbreak for her. But it was too late.

"Yes, David," she said throatily, "make me happy."

His smile lit up the darkness of the room. The breezes whispered as he rose on his elbows and buried his face between her breasts, kissing the firm roundness on either side. Then, one by one, he unfastened the frogs and pulled away the crimson fabric, kissing the smooth white skin as it was revealed to him.

"Oh, sweetheart," he gasped, dropping the blouse to the floor. A white lace bra cradled her breasts, its transparent fragility exposing her rosy nipples. Pleasure thrilled through him as he traced the outline of the trim with his thumb. Her skin was like silk, paler than his, more delicate. She was beautiful.

Her cheeks matched the hue of her nipples as she shrank away, trying to cover herself as she murmured, "I know they're small."

He frowned lovingly, enfolding her hands in his and drawing her nails across his warm, dry lips. "Oh, no, Allison. They're perfect. They're lovely." Releasing her, he covered them with his hands, feeling them with feathery strokes. "They're the bee's knees."

Each light caress made a flame flare inside her. Her back arched against the cool satin and she began to tremble as the fire built. He was magnificent, looming over her with the moon in his hair and magic in his fingers. He overwhelmed her with his great height and his virility; her body was no longer her own, but his, and she wanted him to do all the wonderful things she knew he would.

"It's been a while for you, hasn't it?" he asked. He didn't wait for her reply. Instead, he unhooked the clasp of her bra and pulled it away, unveiling her breasts to his view.

He caught his breath. "Oh, Allison," he said, lowering his head.

His lips encircled first one nipple and then the other, teasing them into taut little points that spoke of her growing desire. He sucked like a child and like a lover, fingers gathering up the soft swells and working the sensitive flesh as he licked every inch of it. He moved slowly, languidly, as if there were no urgency for him, but Allison could feel his hands shaking, his body prodding him toward release.

He groaned, gathering her up in his arms. His entire body was trembling.

"It's okay if you can't . . . wait," she whispered, feeling shy in spite of the wildness that was surging like waves within her. His chest was just inches above her own and she longed for him to crush her against it, melding the two of them together in searing passion. Her very being yearned for it.

His eyes danced, deep amber meeting clear blue crystal. "I've done my waiting," he said. "I want to savor my reward."

His words thrilled her. She put her arms around his neck, the ends of his sleek hair brushing her knuckles. He smelled clean and spicy and his skin was like polished rock. The muscles in the back of his neck were thick cords. She drank in all the details with her detective's sharp senses, reveling in them, discovering all the separate delights that together comprised David, the man that the fog and a missing Shar-Pei had brought into her life.

Clinging to him, she arched her back and lifted herself away from the bed, brushing her nipples against the mat of hair on his chest. He groaned as he fanned his hand against her back and pulled her closer, flattening her breasts against him as he melded her mouth against his.

She parted her lips. Groaning deep in his throat, he accepted her invitation, his tongue dueling with hers. He sat upright, pulling her with him, holding her so tightly, she had to fight to breathe. His hands flew up and down her body, cupping her breasts, her shoulders, diving into the small of her back.

"We need to get rid of these pants," he growled. He held her away and worked at the zipper, easing her back onto her elbows as he snaked them off.

A triangle of white lace tied with mauve ribbons greeted his eyes, and he sat back on his heels for a moment, stirred by her petite beauty. He touched the center of the triangle, then molded the gently rising mound to his hand, easing her thighs apart.

A flush crept from her lower belly to her breasts, darkening her nipples to a deep crimson. It crawled over her neck and lodged itself in her cheeks and forehead. To him she looked like tinted porcelain, and he vowed silently that he would treat her with as much care. She was so small compared to him that he feared he would be too rough and hurt her.

His fingers trembled as he untied the mauve ribbons. His breath was a sharp hiss as her feminine loveliness was exposed to his masculine appreciation.

" 'How fair and how pleasant art thou, O love, for delights!' " he whispered.

In the shadows he looked like a king, like David of the Bible murmuring honeyed words to his beloved. Chandelier rainbows shimmered on Allison's breasts as David knelt between her legs and gathered her in his arms for a kiss. Her hands wrapped around his neck and she kissed him back deeply, rolls of pleasure cascading over her. She undulated in his embrace like a field of peonies swaying in midsummer breezes, blossoming in the radiance of his smile as he filled his hands with her.

Then his smile faded as he moved lover. " 'I am come into my garden,' " he said, sighing as his fingers found the dainty cleft between her legs. He fondled her as if he were stroking something rare and priceless.

Incredible pleasure throbbed where he touched, welling up inside the core of her womanhood and pulsating outward in spirals of sensation. She couldn't describe the feeling, even as she gave herself up to it—tension, heat, anticipation, a heady dizziness combined with a sharp jolt of erotic electricity.

"Allison," he breathed, his voice rolling over her. Her breath quickened as a new tension ignited within her, blurring her senses until sight and sound and feeling were all one—a yearning lust, a mindless need that engulfed her.

"David!" she cried, thrusting her swollen breasts forward as her hands gripped his forearms. "David, oh, David!"

"Yes, Allison, yes."

Clinging to him, Allison raised herself up and threw back her head. Her face was shiny with perspiration.

"Please, David," she said, "please come inside me now."

"Not yet."

She cried out when he withdrew his hand and leaned forward to kiss her. "More," she begged. "Please, don't stop."

"Ah, Allison, there's such fire beneath your surface." He gathered up a corner of the sheet and daubed her forehead, tracing her wispy eyebrows with his fingers. Then he traced the curves of her breasts, pressing his hand over her heart. It was hammering against her rib cage.

She writhed beneath him. "Don't toy with me, dammit," she said through clenched teeth. "Please, don't tease me."

He dropped the sheet and lowered his head to the small delta of ebony.

"All right, love, I won't," he whispered.

He drank deeply of her, branding her with his tongue, losing himself in the honeyed aroma of her womanliness. Allison went rigid beneath him, then began to pant uncontrollably.

"Oh, David, it's about to happen!" she cried. "Please, David, I want you with me!"

"Yes, love, yes." He raised himself up on his knees and poised himself between her legs. "Yes, Allison."

Then he slid into her, joining their bodies, shuddering as Allison reared up from the bed and clung to him. Her head fell back, her lips pulled away from her teeth, and she whimpered in sweet agony.

I'm going to fly apart, she thought as he probed inside

her. He's huge. He's filling me up. I'm on fire everywhere. I'm going to burst into flame, into a million
pieces.

Never had she felt like this. She was in a frenzy, out of
control. There was a roaring in her ears that drowned
out all other sounds, a heat in her body that only served
to heighten the delirious joy that wracked her.

"Can you take more, my love?" David murmured.

She realized he'd been holding back. Unable to speak,
she nodded, and he thrust into her with the full force of
his maleness.

It triggered the culmination for her. Her entire body
tensed, hovering on the brink, reaching for the apex.
Her flesh strained to contain her passion, and she trembled from head to toe as she flew past the veils of delight
and reaching and joining.

"David!" She burst free, flinging herself to new
heights of ecstasy filled with sparks and comets and
David all around her. He was moaning her name,
kissing her everywhere, touching her, caressing her,
holding her as she climaxed in a frenzy of wonderful,
unimaginable pleasure.

Gradually she became aware that tears were streaming down her cheeks and that David's back was arched
as he pumped the last of his seed into her. She tasted
the salt and smelled the earthy scent of lovemaking.
Sighing, she relaxed her grip on him and sank onto the
bed.

All at once she felt shy as David flopped his head forward and opened his eyes, staring down at her. She covered her breasts, but he gently forced her hands away
and kissed each love-reddened nipple. Then he rolled
onto his back and scooted her into the crook of his arm.

She saw the pulse in his neck and the dampness on
the curls of his hair. Both of them were panting, gulping
for air. Neither spoke.

David put his other arm around her, cuddling her,
and kissed her temple. He was filled with emotion. His
throat was tight and his soul yearned to tell her how he

felt about her. But he refrained, knowing that it would ruin the moment for her.

"So, Bathsheba," he murmured, seeking to break the spell of wonder that held him, "whaddaya think?"

Chuckling, she found his hand and squeezed it hard. "Thank you," she whispered. "That was the most wonderful experience I've ever had."

He felt dangerously close to tears and couldn't risk speaking. He could only hug her then and tenderly kiss her forehead.

They lay quietly for a while, clasping and unclasping each other's hands. Then David's fingers grew limp and he began to snore softly, throwing his arm over his eyes and sighing in his sleep.

But Allison, drained as she was, was too exhilarated even to doze. Holding his hand, she stared wide-eyed at the crystal chandelier until daylight stained it with vivid color that it threw in riotous splashes against the far wall. Then she slept.

Seven

Allison giggled, still half-asleep. He was tickling her toes, licking them with his hot, wet tongue. Squinting against the bright sunlight that streamed through the curtains, she wiggled, batting playfully at him in an attempt to make him stop.

"That's enough!" Laughing, she caught her heel in the folds of the sheets, and as she tried to free it, he began to nibble on the big toe of her other foot.

"Stop!" she shrieked. She sat up and scooted out of the way, but he lunged for the delectable morsels.

"Hey, truce!" She knelt on the bed and waved her finger at him. "You make a lousy bed partner!"

Bulldog Drummond, her Boston terrier, squatted back on his haunches and barked at her. Then he skittered along the mattress and nuzzled her hand.

"I thought I locked you out last night," she said, scratching him behind the ears. "Has everyone else escaped too?"

He panted and tried to nip her fingers. "Oh, you're naughty!" She gave him a little swat and lifted him off the bed.

David stood in the doorway, drying his hair. A pale yellow towel was draped around his waist, slung low on his hips. He smiled to himself as he watched Allison cavorting like a lithe Diana, the Grecian goddess of the hunt usually portrayed in the company of her hunting dogs. Unselfconsciously, she flopped over the side of the bed, dangling her fingers, laughing when the terrier began to lick them.

You wonderful lady, he thought, his chest tightening. You angel.

Not wanting to destroy the moment, he stood quietly, admiring the soft curves of her body—the proud, jutting breasts, the willowy hips and legs. Her hair was a sexy tangle of curls that bobbed and nodded as she pretended to pounce on the dog, lunging and retreating on all fours, her high, tinkling laugh a delight in the early morning stillness.

My wonderful lady, he thought, adjusting the towel and daubing the hairs on his chest. Only she wasn't his. She didn't want to be. And if she even suspected he was thinking like this, she'd probably ask him to kindly leave the room—via the second-story window.

"Oh, you're a bad boy!" Allison said, laughing as Drummond growled and barked. "So bad!"

So his best play was to act casual, David decided, as if they still weren't involved with each other. As if he didn't care about her so much that he wanted to gather her up in his arms and ask her to . . . to . . .

He swallowed. Oh, God, the guys were right. It happens to all of us. I want to get married, dammit!

"Oh, Drummond! You big lug!"

Calm down, he told himself. You hardly know her. Hell, you've dated other women for months and months and you never lost your reason before. No sense going off the deep end after a couple of weeks.

"Damn right," he said under his breath.

Allison looked up, startled. "Oh, I didn't see you there," she murmured. modestly drawing the sheet over herself. David found the gesture incredibly touching. All at once she was shy and girlish as her blue eyes swept over his nearly naked form, an enchanting blush crowning her cheeks.

"I just got out of the shower," he said. He toyed with

the edge of the towel, his mind racing. But he did want to marry her, he thought. He really did. He blinked. "I didn't realize you were awake." Then, retaining some of his composure, he added with a wolfish swagger, "Or I'd have asked you to join me."

The blush deepened. Oh, darling, sweet Allison. What could he do to make her his?

"The terrier woke me up," she told him as Bulldog Drummond scrambled from underneath the bed and hurried to inspect the stranger in his mistress's bedroom. "He's used to sleeping with me."

"Lucky dog."

She chuckled, which surprised him. There was a lusty tinge to the sound that was totally unexpected. Chaste pet detective or playful sex kitten—which was the real Allison? Or was she both?

Just then Hercule Parrot soared into the room, dive-bombing toward Drummond—and David. The pooch squealed and ran behind David, who ducked out of the way. Giving up, Hercule flew away, performing a few aerial pirouettes before he perched on the headboard. He bobbed up and down like a pogo stick, cocking his head at Allison.

"Shame on you, Hercule!" she admonished. "You know better than to do that!"

"Who done it? Who done it?" chirped the parrot.

Allison put a hand on her hip, the other holding her sheet in place. "Don't pretend you don't understand me," she cautioned. "That'll get you two to five in the pen outside."

"Cheese, it's the cops! Cheese, it's the cops!" the parrot chanted brightly. "Who done it?"

"I'd say we done it," David drawled, his bare feet padding on the hardwood floor. Allison's back was to him, a long, smooth plain of flesh ending in two dimples above the hidden roundness of her bottom. He ached to have his fingers slide down it, to wrap himself around her and plant kisses in the cascade of ringlets and tendrils that brushed the nape of her neck. He'd planned to be at the office by eight, but already in his mind he was phoning in to say he would be delayed.

"And if I have anything to say about it," he went on, "we're going to do it again. Right now."

Allison turned around to face him, spiraling the sheet around herself. Now she looked like a Grecian nymph—or innocent Miranda, in Shakespeare's *The Tempest*, catching her first glimpse of a man.

" 'Oh, brave new world that hath such people in't,' " he said softly, sitting beside her on the bed. Slowly he drew the sheet away, covering her with his hands instead. "Detective Jones, get rid of the witnesses so we can recommit the crime."

She inhaled sharply, swooning beneath his touch. Their lovemaking had been like nothing else in her entire life. David was like no one else. Even now she was hypnotized by his expert caresses, the piercing gaze from eyes dark and impenetrable as obsidian. Windows to the soul . . . What a soul this man must have, she thought dizzily.

"Crime?" she managed to say. "What crime?"

"Of passion."

Passion only? She looked at his sienna hands cupping her breasts, pinching her budding nipples into a thrill of pleasure-pain, and struggled not to reveal the questions in her eyes. For her they had committed not a crime, but an act of love. Even now, feeling David's breath at the hollow in her throat, her heart filled with a deep, abiding devotion that would probably send him scooting down the stairway if he knew about it.

Damn, she thought, shivering as David ran a finger down her stomach. She was falling in love with the most unsuitable man in the world for her. The King of the Bachelors, no less. She must be insane.

"Allison?" David said, peering through the lustrous fringes of lashes that ringed his eyes. He abandoned her breasts and cupped her chin in his hands, tilting back her head so he could study her features. "Are you all right?"

"Sure," she replied brightly, shrugging. "I'm fine." She softened, letting the false cheer slip from her voice. "It was wonderful, David."

They regarded each other. Love me, each thought. Love me only. Want me only. Be my one and only.

Don't hurt me.

"Rosebud, Rosebud!" Hercule warbled. "Here's looking at you, kid!"

"Get rid of the spectators," David said huskily, stroking her neck. "I want to perform privately."

His words deflated her. Perform? Is that how he saw the most shattering event of her life? As an exercise of his macho prowess?

He was becoming more aroused. The sight of his masculine fullness, growing because of her, excited her as well. Her body began to prepare itself for him, to moisten and warm and ripen. Each place he touched, each part of her he gazed on, expanded to a new awareness of sensuality. She wanted desperately to blot out her thoughts and lie back on the tangled sheets, offering herself to him. She had a vision of the two of them as mystical pagans worshiping one another's bodies, sacrificing their apartness, daring, in spite of their apprehensions, to unite in the throes of rapturous oblivion. To mate, to die and live again, free of doubt, and worry, and fear . . .

David bent his head to her breast, sucking the taut crimson nipple. "Oh, yes," he purred. "Want me the way I want you."

No, her mind protested. She couldn't want him like that—with no emotion attached. And each time she slept with him, she'd become more emotional about him—and he'd be untouched. And in the end . . .

"I really have to get going," she said brusquely. "I have a long day today. I have to find a tortoise named Festina Lente."

With a sharp shake of her head, she pulled away from the force of his nearness. Gliding out of his reach, she kept her back to him as she walked to the closet and pulled out her bathrobe. Her hands were shaking, her body crying out for his.

"I can cook you breakfast," she offered, her voice quavering. She couldn't let him go just yet. Perhaps she could build something more between them than shared pleasure in the bedroom—laughter and understanding and mutual affection.

Oh, say it, she told herself. You want him to *love* you too. But with a man like David, was that possible?

David started to accept her offer, but stopped himself. He mustn't intrude on her. He couldn't make his visits a burden, though heaven knows right now it was a struggle to remind himself of that. All he wanted was to throw her down and make love to her.

"Naw, that's all right," he said casually. "I'll pick something up on my way to the office. You just go ahead and pretend I'm not here."

Pretend he wasn't there? What did he think she was, a robot who could turn her feelings on and off when it pleased him?

Welcome back to the singles' scene, she thought miserably. Isn't it fun?

"All right," she said, squaring her shoulders and lifting her chin. "I'll be downstairs if you need me."

Need you? he thought. If you only knew.

She trudged downstairs, leaving him to dress. As she took each step, her thighs and buttocks ached from the exertion of the night before. Such fierce, wild lovemaking! He was like an animal when he was aroused, a primitive savage—

Fierce, wild *sex*, Allison, she corrected herself. For him there had been no love involved.

In the kitchen she put on the teakettle and stood near the stove watching the gas flame. Tears of disappointment and humiliation began to well in her eyes. She should never have done it, never in a million years. She shouldn't have climbed into the Lincoln that day in Chinatown. She shouldn't have—

Hindsight's a marvelous thing, she reminded herself. It was too late now.

"Well, I guess I'll be going," David said from the doorway. The jacket of his white suit was slung over his shoulder, the tie dangling around his neck. He hesitated, hoping she'd repeat her invitation to breakfast. At least she could offer him a cup of coffee.

A trio of mews stole into the silence. The M&M&Ms bounded up to David. Magnum hopped onto his shoe and began to bat at the hem of his trouser.

"Hi, guys," David said, and reared back for a tremendous sneeze. The kittens scattered like feathers.

He laughed sheepishly, drawing a handkerchief from his pocket and patting his nose. "I think I'm allergic to your roommates," he told her. "Maybe we'd better start going to my house."

Allison, terrified she was going to break down in front of him, said nothing. She concentrated on measuring fragrant, chocolate-colored beans into a grinder. They filled the air with a spicy scent.

"So. I'm off," David said, trying to peer over her shoulder to see her face.

Reaching for the filters in the cupboard, she managed to say, "Okay. See you." She closed her eyes as he paused, turned on his heel, and walked out of the house.

The first tear trickled down her cheek just as she heard him start his car and pull away.

David had planned to wait two days before he called her. A chauffeured Packard Custom Super Clipper—1947, he thought automatically, Henney body, one-hundred-forty-eight-inch wheelbase, a dream on whitewalls—had been dispatched with a dozen long-stemmed red roses later on that confusing morning. He'd paused over the card, smiling grimly because none of his glib bachelor phrases could express his feelings, and because he was afraid to tell her how he felt, anyway. So he had simply signed his name.

Then he'd planned to leave her alone for a while. He

wanted to prove he wouldn't try to dominate her, take over her life. That must have been what was bothering her. He knew how suffocated one could feel when a night's passion was spent and you were left with the strange and awkward rituals of morning-after politeness that threw off your routine. It could be irritating to have to wait to use your own bathroom, or to discover that you had a talker on your hands when all you wanted was to grope for a cup of coffee and the paper and try to wake up. Allison must be a groper, he decided.

So he would let her know he understood and wasn't planning to upset her patterns. Two days would make that statement. Forty-eight hours.

But after twenty-four he couldn't keep his fingers off the phone. She was like a heady drug that he couldn't get enough of. She was in his bloodstream. The mere thought of her was like the afterglow of a glass or two of fine brandy.

In the end he'd succumbed, and had capped off his surrender by inviting her to dinner. And now, as he opened the wine to let it breathe, he heard the limo he'd sent to pick her up pulling into the driveway.

He stopped to check everything. Candlelight, wine, mellow jazz instead of his usual earsplitting rock music. He was California casual in a blue and white striped rugby shirt, jeans, and cowboy boots. The maid had been in, so the place was clean. Everything was as perfect as he could get it.

"Showtime, King," he murmured as the car engine died. He checked his hair in the mirror and laughed at his reflection. "Who'd ever have guessed you'd be nervous about a woman?" he asked it. He looked down at his bare ring finger and rubbed it. Who'd ever have guessed?

Allison was stunned by the size of his house. When he'd told her he lived in Pacific Heights, she was prepared for a large apartment in one of the posh, newer buildings that etched the nighttime skyline. But the chauffeur brought her to a French Provincial mansion just two blocks, he told her, from the home of the French consul himself.

It was three stories tall, with dormer windows and a roof that looked as if it might actually be slate. Sitting at the top of a hill, it commanded an impressive view of the bay side of the city. Well-trimmed bushes sided the front door, on which hung a large lion's head knocker. It wasn't at all the kind of home she'd imagined for him.

The chauffeur escorted her to the door. Just as they reached it, David opened it and drew her into his arms, tenderly brushing her lips.

"Hello," he said, admiring her. She'd dressed for the occasion in a black velvet dress with padded shoulders and a keyhole neckline. There were black polka dots on her seamed nylons, and stiletto heels with ankle straps completed the ensemble. She was a new woman to him, sophisticated and mysterious, the antithesis of the laughing sprite who'd teased the Boston terrier in all the glory of her perfect nakedness.

Ah, Allison, you're many women in one, he thought. Would he ever get to know them all?

"Hubba hubba," he said finally, leading her into the house.

"Well, I'd say so too," she responded, eyes widening.

This was more like the house she'd pictured for him. After seeing the exterior, walking into the living room was like crossing a time warp. A huge field of silver-gray carpet was dotted with groupings of starkly modern wooden chairs and tables of abstract design. Two leather couches faced each other, each dominated by a freestanding metal lamp that curved above it. The walls were decorated with splashy acrylics and oils, and what appeared to be an original Leroy Neiman of a man on a motorcycle. A huge sound system covered an entire wall, silver and black cubes positioned around a wide-screen TV.

She caught her reflection in a smoked-glass mirror and laughed at her own astonishment.

"I don't know why I'm so surprised," she said,

accepting a glass of white wine from him. "It's exactly the kind of setting I'd put you in."

David picked up a chrome box and flicked a switch. Instantly the lights dimmed and the music volume inched up until he pressed the switch again.

He looked at her over the edge of his wineglass. "I'm going to take that as a compliment," he drawled.

"Oh, yes," she said, "please do."

"Would you like to see the rest of the house?"

His bedroom, she thought instantly, and took another sip of wine. "Perhaps in a little while," she murmured.

His eyes narrowed, but he said nothing. Gesturing for her to sit, he joined her on the couch that faced sliding glass doors.

A panoramic view of the sunset on the water shimmered before her. The sky blazed with iridescent oranges and scarlets, glazing the bay below with turquoise and gold. Like chains of copper, the Golden Gate sparkled in the last moments of full sunlight. Gulls wheeled in silhouette, disappearing among salmon-colored clouds. A tugboat hoot echoed over the water.

The wine was delicious. So was the look and smell of David, who propped his feet on the coffee table and put his arm around her. His profile was dappled with sunglow as he leaned back and sighed with contentment.

He closed his eyes for a moment, then opened them quickly and turned to her, setting down his glass.

"Did I tell you what I got in the mail yesterday?" he asked, grinning. She shook her head. "A wedding invitation from Raphael."

She fingered the lip of her goblet. "A *wedding* invitation?" she asked doubtfully. "Who's he marrying?"

"Well, actually, he's 'choosing to bond.' With Patrick, a dancer with the San Francisco Ballet. They're going to have a ceremony at the Metropolitan Community Church."

She smiled, remembering Raphael's delight when they'd returned Bruce Lee. He was a dear, kindhearted soul—and he was in love. "Well, I'm happy for him. I hope they'll be happy together."

David nodded. "Me too. When I first met you, I thought you and Raphael . . ." He winked at her. "You know, they want a 'real' wedding, but I guess this is the closest they can get legally."

"A real wedding," she mused, seeing again how elegant David had looked in his formal clothes and gloves. "Janet told me she and Hunter are going to get married soon. He's been hinting about asking her and she's already window-shopping for a dress."

David rose suddenly, running a hand through his hair. "What is it with everybody, wanting to get married all of a sudden?" he asked, taking a deep draft of wine. "Is it something in the water or what?"

Allison could do nothing but persuade a grimace to struggle into a smile and shrug.

"I remember the good old sixties," he went on, walking toward the kitchen. Allison rose and followed him. His back was hunched and he gesticulated with his wineglass as he talked. "Nobody would be caught dead getting married! It was even frowned upon to be monogamous."

"Terribly *outré*," Allison agreed.

"And now everyone wants to do it."

She allowed him to pour her some more wine, watching the liquid stream into her glass so that he couldn't see the look on her face. Her strained smile kept slipping. What did you expect from a guy like this? she asked herself. You knew what was going on.

"Surely not everybody," she croaked.

David tossed off his second glass and poured himself a third. He didn't speak for a moment. Don't blow it, King, he warned. Don't scare her off.

"Well, of course not," he said brightly. "It's the farthest thing from *my* mind." He looked at her expectantly.

"Oh, mine too," she assured him, the words nearly catching in her throat.

Allison, don't be ridiculous, she chided. You *can't* be thinking that he and you—that he would ever—

"What does Festina Lente mean?" David asked. He pulled a cloth off two thick steaks and turned on his oven broiler. With a deftness that impressed her, he slid each one onto a two-pronged fork and deposited it on the grill.

"Make haste slowly," she replied.

He smiled as he shut the broiler door and opened the refrigerator. "And that's the name of a turtle?"

She nodded. "A tortoise. He belongs to a Latin professor."

"I like it," he said, putting his arms around her and kissing the crown of her head. "It has a certain seductive ring to it."

"Turtles are seductive creatures," she replied, listening to his heartbeat. "They like to lie in the sun, barely moving, snapping at flies." She closed her eyes when she realized she'd made a double entendre.

"Make haste slowly," David repeated. "Do you want to make some haste?"

She breathed in slowly as his arms tightened, urging her against his chest. His heart was beating faster. "The steaks will burn."

"Not if we're hasty."

"Haste makes waste," she pointed out.

"He who hesitates is lost."

"Fools rush in—"

"Oh, sweetheart, I don't care how I get there," he said, his voice low and deep. "Just let me in."

Fat from the steaks made the broiler fire sizzle. Speaking against his shoulder, she said, "It's probably time to turn over. Turn them over," she corrected herself quickly.

He sighed. "All right, Ally-oop. I see where your priorities lie. Stomach over gonads. My mother always told me the way to a woman's bikini underwear was through her taste buds."

She kept her gaze on the broiler door. He had said nothing about her heart.

The steaks were ready in short order. David slid them onto a platter with a flourish, but when Allison reached out her hands to carry it to the table, he waved her away and said, "No, let Gort do it."

"Huh?"

"Watch," David said, grinning as he picked up another little silver box and aimed it in the direction of what Allison assumed was a pantry.

The door swung open. A metal figure as tall as Allison whirred toward them. Its body was streamlined, its legs actually one long, stable, shiny stem with wheels under it. The arms at its sides ended in nothing but a pair of smooth hooks. Though it had a contoured face, there were no eyes or other features to speak of.

"Gort, klaatu barada nickto," David said, and the thing whirred over to the counter where the platter of steaks lay. Its arms bent at right angles and it swiveled its head in David's direction.

"Baringa," David said after placing the platter on its arms.

The robot made a slight turn and headed toward the table.

Allison scooted out of the way, since obviously it wasn't going to go around her. She clapped her hands in delight as it stopped at the table's edge and set the platter down.

"How'd you get it to do that?" she asked excitedly.

Smiling, David pressed a button and the robot's head turned in Allison's direction. "Hel-lo Al-li-son," it intoned. "How's-a-about-a lit-tle kiss."

Her hands flew to her face. "It sounds Swedish! Oh, David, it's amazing! How did you make it say my name?"

"I'm a mad genius," he said. "Gort, klaatu barada nickto."

The robot whirred and clicked, then turned around and followed David back into the kitchen.

"It knows what you're saying," she said faintly, impressed.

"Voice recognition," he agreed. "A few commands programmed in. It's simple, really."

"It doesn't look simple to me."

"That's only because you don't understand it." He drew her into his arms. "There's a lot you don't understand, Detective Jones."

She leaned her head back to peer up at him, nearly ending up in a back bend. "Like what?" she demanded.

"Like this," he said softly.

They kissed. David grew more ardent, crushing her against his body, until the robot beeped and nearly sent Allison through the ceiling.

"It's reminding me it's still on," David explained, "so the batteries won't wear out." He set a tray over Gort's hook-hands and placed a glass salad bowl on top of it.

"Wouldn't it be easier to carry things to the table ourselves?" Allison asked, following behind with two bowls of sliced fruit laced with honey.

David threw a sheepish grin at her over his shoulder. "Sure. But it wouldn't be as much fun. Besides, Gort cost me a fortune. I have to get some use out of him."

"Did you build him?"

"Hel-lo Al-li-son," the robot said.

"No. I'm not a tinkerer, just a gadget freak." He watched appreciatively as Gort slid the tray toward the table. "I love the future, don't you? I can't wait for—No! Stop!" he cried, leaping forward.

"Hel-lo Al-li-son," repeated the robot, and dumped the salad bowl on the floor.

They cleaned up the mess—with an old-fashioned broom—and banished Gort to his lair. As they ate, they spoke of inconsequential things—news articles and TV shows, the night a rock group had hired all David's limos to ferry guests from the Cow Palace to a huge party in a warehouse two blocks away. Allison told him about old Mrs. Mackelhenny, who picked up more strays than she did and was loathe to part with any of them, even when Allison was working for one of their owners.

"So I trade," she told him. "If I can't find parents for Magnum, Mannix, and McCloud, I'll give them to Mrs. Mackelhenny in exchange for someone else's pet."

"Have you ever thought of becoming a sports team manager? You could do wonders for the Giants," David teased.

It was a good dinner. David was charming, an excellent conversationalist who really listened to what she had to say. She felt a bridge growing between them as they built up a common pool of stories and small secrets and jokes. They were less strangers than they had been before.

After a dessert of mango ice cream and Italian vanilla cookies, served by human hands, she started to help him clear the table.

"No, don't bother," he said. His lids grew heavy and languid in a decidedly come-hither invitation. "I don't want you tiring yourself out."

"Really, it's no trouble," she began, but he laid a firm hand on her arm as he took a coffee cup from her.

"Just relax," he told her. "Take yourself on a tour of my house." And make a slight detour into the bedroom, his eyes suggested.

"All right," she said, pretending not to notice his sultry look.

The lights dimmed automatically as she wandered through the living room and down a hall. Behind her, she heard the whoosh of the faucet as he rinsed and stacked the dishes. The corridor walls were lined with signed acrylics of classic cars, and she wondered if David had had portraits painted of his fleet. It struck her as funny at first, but then she thought, why not? She knew plenty of people who treasured paintings of their dogs and cats—why not cars?

Most of the doors were open. She peered in one and saw a bathroom done completely in white. It adjoined a huge master suite decorated in earth tones and dominated by a huge bed with a mahogany headboard, inside of which were enough controls to navigate a spaceship. The bedspread was folded at the foot of the bed and one corner of the shiny beige sheets—silk, she thought—was drawn back, as if to welcome her to the premises.

A warmth spread through her and she went on to the next door, which was shut. And which, of course, she opened.

It was a bachelor's den done in dark wood with another leather couch. Obviously a private retreat, and she knew it was probably impolite to examine it.

But sometimes detectives had to be impolite to solve mysteries. For her David King was very much an enigma.

But as she moved through the room, she was sorry she'd decided to snoop. Everywhere was evidence of David's fierce devotion to a free-swinging bachelor life: photographs of him with various women, all beautiful in the Lady Godiva style; an erotic oil; a hologram of a Ferrari; not one, not two, but three black telephone books, one of which included her phone number; and a years-old, framed newspaper piece from a women's organization decrying one David Robert King as November's "Premier Male Chauvinist Pig."

In the bookcase were books on massage and wine, directories to fine nightspots, gadget catalogues, classic car books, worn copies of *The Sensuous Man*, *The Joy of Sex* and, of all things, *How to Pick Up Girls*.

She slumped, perching on the edge of a small desk that held a computer and a stack of diskettes. There was a message machine beside the stack, and on top of it was a note pad embossed with a logo of a limousine and the words "King Limo" beneath it. Under the date David had scribbled a list of women's names, with Allison's circled. Had he struck out with all the others before he'd asked her to dinner?

Get out of here, Allison, she told herself, running down the list. Don't stay in this room or you're going to spoil everything.

He knew two Karens, both a Laurie and a Laura, and some exotic lady called Angelique. At least no one else was named Allison. That must make it a little tougher on him to remember not to cry out the incorrect name . . .

"Oh, Allison, don't be dumb," she muttered, biting her thumbnail.

But self-preservation wasn't dumb. She tapped the list with numb fingers, then swept her gaze across the books, the photographs, the oil painting of a nude woman reading a book on a sandy beach.

It would be dumber to pretend none of this bothered her, that she didn't mind being one of a cast of thousands. After all, not even Bette Davis would be able to cope with it. Jeanette MacDonald would just die. Bacall would tell him to give her back her whistle.

Tears welled in her eyes as she listened to David's tuneless whistling in the kitchen. She should have stuck to her guns. She should have sworn off men. Damn.

Axiom: Men leave Allison Jones. Fact: David King was a man. Conclusion—

Get out now, Allison. It'll hurt worse later.

One tear made the great escape. She wiped it away angrily and rose from the desk. Smoothing her dress, she rubbed her eyes again and tried to clear her throat. It had begun to ache and there was an awful buzzing in her head that made it impossible to think.

She didn't need to think. She already knew what she had to do.

He was cleaning the kitchen countertops with a sponge when she walked up behind him. They seemed as small as dollhouse furnishings compared to his great height and large hands. He was humming now, occasionally singing "true love," and she vaguely recognized the melody as one that had blared from the stereo in his car.

We don't have enough in common anyway, anyway,

she told herself, watching his body move inside his jeans. He was a poor choice from the beginning.

Choice? Had she really had one?

"All finished," David announced, wringing out the sponge. He turned around and held out his arms. "How about a reward kiss for me for having done all the dirty work around this joint?"

Not all of it, my love, she thought, studying his face for what she knew would be the last time.

"David, I have to go home," she whispered, emotion robbing her of her voice. She clenched her hands into a tight ball.

He looked at her, his smile fading into an expression of concern. "Why, honey? Don't you feel well?"

She shook her head, lowering her head to hide the tears.

"Are you catching something?" He bent down and placed a palm over her forehead. "You don't feel feverish, but then, my hands have been in warm water. Do you want some aspirin?"

She covered his hand with hers, feeling electricity course through her. They were good hands, muscular and warm. She could feel the veins beneath the skin as he squeezed her fingers.

It wasn't his fault, she reminded herself. He had done nothing to deserve her anger. He'd always been honest. She hadn't.

Good-bye, my love, her heart wept as she clutched his hand more tightly. Take care.

"No, David, I just need to go home. If you'll tell the chauffeur—"

"Nonsense," he said brusquely, his worry evident. "I'll drive you home myself."

The phone rang. Barry answered it in her office while Allison opened a bag he'd brought in and examined some funny-looking turnbuckles and a spool of fishing line.

"No, she's not here right now," she heard Barry say, and her heart skipped a beat. It must be David. Again.

It was cowardly of her not to face him, she knew, but she was afraid she'd cave in and agree to see him if she did. In the two weeks since the night she'd gone to his house, she'd often thought of taking his call and agreeing to a reunion. But being with him again would only postpone the heartbreak.

He'd been hounding her night and day. First there were lots of questions about how she felt, about going to a doctor. He'd offered to drive her to one himself, offered to pay if she couldn't afford it. Then he tried to get Barry to tell him what was going on. He asked if Allison was dating someone else, if she was happy, and so on. Barry was always evasive, but that didn't seem to stop him.

"Maybe Karen, Laurie, Karen, Laura, and Angelique are all busy," she said, sighing, and idly twisting a turnbuckle.

No, that wasn't fair. She knew he cared about her—in his limited bachelor's way. She closed her eyes, remembering their night of passion, missing him more than she would have thought possible.

In the next room Barry was saying good-bye to the caller.

He ambled into the living room. She licked her lips and asked, "Was it him?"

He picked up two turnbuckles and hooked them together, then a third, a fourth, a fifth. Taking the sixth from Allison, he shook his head. She slumped inside.

"Naw, it was just my climbing instructor. He's changing the day to next Monday. I figured you didn't want to talk to him."

Sighing again, she nodded.

"Hey, I can stay home if you can't handle it," he said. "It was your idea for me to go in the first place."

"No, no, go ahead," she said quickly. It had taken a lot of convincing to get Barry to take a mountaineering class, and this trip to the mountains was his first crack at something that wasn't man-made and perfectly perpendicular to the ground.

David didn't call at all that weekend. Allison figured he'd given up, and waved good-bye to Barry at dawn on Monday with a relieved, if grieving, heart.

But at seven the phone rang. Allison hesitated before answering it, almost switching on the answering machine.

"But what if it's important? What if it's a client?" she asked aloud, chewing on her thumbnail. "What if it's somebody like Raphael, falling to pieces because his dog is missing? Or Maribeth in Europe?"

Besides, David had never phoned this early in the morning. She was probably safe.

Taking a deep breath, she picked up the receiver.

"Hello?" she said in a clear, steady voice.

She was right. It was important.

"Allison?" David said. "I need you. It's an emergency."

Eight

Allison gripped the receiver with both hands. "David, what's wrong?" she cried. "Are you all right?"

His voice sounded tired and drawn. "My dog is missing. I can't find him anywhere."

She sat behind her desk, drawing her bathrobe over her legs and picking up a pencil. "You don't have a dog," she said.

"I just got one. To console myself."

Over her? she wondered. She swallowed and began to doodle on a note pad, scrawling "David, David, David" in flowing script inside the magnifying glass in her logo. Her heart was racing and she drank in every syllable he uttered. It was so wonderful to hear his voice that she had trouble focusing on exactly what he was saying.

But what he was saying didn't make sense.

"You're allergic to animal hair," she pointed out.

"No, just cat hair. I went to the doctor and checked. Please, Ally-oop, he's all alone somewhere. He's probably scared to death."

It was the call to duty. Allison leaned forward in her chair and pulled off the used page of paper. Starting fresh, she sighed and said, "All right. Give me a description."

"Oh, thanks," David breathed. "You don't know how frantic I've been."

Tears sprang to her eyes. She missed him so much. She touched her hand to her tousled hair, as if he were there to see it, and said gently, "The description, David."

David paused. "I don't know what to say."

"Let's start with his breed."

"St. Bernard."

She knit her brows. "A St. Bernard? David, you can't keep a big dog like that in the city!" She heard him huff and decided this was no time for a lecture. After all, she shouldn't be keeping all those animals in her house, either. The trouble was, there was nowhere else for them to go.

"All right," she said soothingly, "a St. Bernard. How old?"

"How old?" David echoed. "I don't know!"

"Didn't the pet shop tell you?"

"The pet shop," he mused, then replied, "I bought him from a private party. But he's about, oh, two-and-a-half feet tall."

"That small? It's a male?"

"Yes."

"Then he must be a puppy," she said, writing everything down. "What are his markings?"

Another pause. "Oh, your usual St. Bernard markings, I suppose."

"Red with white or white with red?"

"Damn, I don't know."

He was really worried; she could tell by the strain in his voice. Her professionalism took hold of her. She almost forgot it was David she was speaking to. "All right, let's start over. Is there anything to distinguish him from other St. Bernards? A special mark perhaps? An unusual way of walking?"

"He's got two black stripes down his forehead to his nose," David said triumphantly.

She scratched her nose with the pencil and crossed her legs. "Are you sure? That's very strange."

"I'm sure."

"Okay. Does he answer to a name?"

"Cujo," he replied quickly.

She chuckled as she wrote it down. "Fine. Is there anything else, David? Does he like people? What does he eat?"

She went on with a list of questions. David's responses were vague and preoccupied, not too much help. But the black stripes would make the dog easy to spot.

"Okay, I'll get right on it," she told him, sorry that the conversation was at an end. Funny, she had day-dreamed about talking to him again, but never had she imagined that this was what they would discuss. Her fanciful thoughts had turned into scenes from all her favorite old movies until David was Bogie and she was Ingrid, and instead of putting her on the plane in Casablanca, he fell to his knees and insisted they get married right away.

"When shall we start searching for him?" David asked.

She was startled by his question. "What do you mean 'we'?"

"Well, he's *my* dog."

Don't, Allison, a voice inside her warned. This time she heeded it. "Oh, no," she said. "Like Philip Marlowe before me, I work alone."

"But—"

"I'll be in touch," she said, and quickly hung up.

Later that day she saw the limo before the limo saw her. It was a long black Lincoln and it kept swimming up and down the streets like a shark searching out its prey. She had no doubt that either David was in it or David had sent it.

She lost it easily. Any good pet detective could lose a tail—or find one.

But David's Cujo was nowhere to be found. She cased his neighborhood, dodging Packards and Bentleys and Lincoln Continentals all the way, interviewing his neighbors and passing out flyers that described the dog and listed her phone number, with the promise of a reward for useful information. To her dismay, she discovered that most of the more nubile Pacific Heighters had designs on the attractive Mr. King. One of them always managed to be watering her lawn in her bikini when he drove one of his cars out of the garage. Another one told her of wild bachelor parties and described how well he kissed.

In the next few days he called several times to check on her progress, each time insisting he be allowed to accompany her. But she continued to go it alone.

The early morning hours were best for sleuthing. Most people were still asleep and lost pets, overwhelmed by the daytime crowds, crept out into the solitude of dawn and began their lonely hunt for food and the trail home.

The earlier, the better. It was barely light out when Allison wandered along the Embarcadero, belting her trench coat against the last remnants of the fog. Derelicts were still snoozing on the benches in the park area across from the bright green cable car parked on a block of cement. The rising sun glittered in the mirrored surfaces of the massive Hyatt Regency, its quasi-pyramid angles deflecting the light like a prism. Beside it, twin towers of offices rose into the clouds.

It was cold. She stamped her feet, longing for a cup of coffee. Why had she come down here anyway? It would be an astounding coincidence if she found Cujo here. But she'd had a hunch in the shower and she always trusted her hunches.

"Yeah, right. Like with David," she said ruefully, stuffing her hands into her pockets.

Then she saw him. Two feet tall, red with white, favoring the right front paw. He sniffed at the cable car and surveyed a trio of sleeping winos, then started to cross the street, heading for the Hyatt.

Allison moved in his direction, neither too fast nor too slowly. As if he sensed her, he began evasive maneuvers, making a beeline for the modern fountain on the other side of the plaza, a maze of cement blocks on which were stenciled the words "Quebec Libre"—the artist's political opinion, not necessarily the city's. A wall of water gushed over a walkway, and it was there that the dog turned around and looked in her direction.

The black stripes! Two of them, right between the eyes. Maintaining a steady, calm pace, she strode toward him.

"Cujo?" she called, her voice warm and friendly. "Cujo? Come here, boy."

He wagged his tail and barked. She smiled encouragingly. "That's right. Come here."

Barking again, he turned away and trotted farther under the path of the waterfall. Allison made a face and minced nearer.

"Come on, sweetheart. Let's go home to David."

He took three steps toward her, one step back. She stood still and let him observe her, trying to appear as unthreatening as possible. Her fedora flirted with the stiff morning wind, but she didn't move to secure it.

"Hey, lady, c'n you spare a quarter?" asked a man. He was one of the winos who'd been asleep on the benches, and somehow he'd managed to creep up behind her. He was raggedy, his face one brown bristle, and he smelled of Red Train wine, which had been Allison's drink of choice during the experimental portion of her youth. She knew from experience that it tasted like diet strawberry soda.

"No," she said, "please go away." An idea suddenly popped into her mind and she half-turned her head. "Wait. Listen, if you can keep an eye on that dog and make sure he doesn't get away, I'll give you a dollar."

"Lessee it," he demanded.

"No. First you have to guard the dog," she said, already starting to walk away.

They would have phones in the Hyatt. As soon as she was out of the St. Bernard's territory, she raced inside.

They had phones; she didn't have a dime. Neither did the few workers preparing for the morning. Nothing was open. No one had change. She was sure she'd just passed into the Twilight Zone.

"Damn," she muttered. It was unforgivably stupid of her. She always carried dimes and nickels for just this purpose. But today she didn't even have bus fare home.

She'd blame it on David, she decided. She'd been too preoccupied with him.

Meanwhile, where to get some dimes?

The cavernous lobby of the hotel boasted two fountains: a huge sphere floating above a pool as smooth and dark as black glass, and a meandering stream, in a rectangular box, that gurgled oriental-style over small ginger-colored stones.

In that stream people had been making wishes. Nickles, pennies, and dimes gleamed under the moving water.

"Eureka!" Allison cried, falling to her knees and straining to salvage some of the sunken treasure. But, as often happened, she was too small to successfully complete her mission.

"Damn," she muttered again, and, without a moment's hesitation, climbed into the fountain—boots, coat, and all—and slogged toward the nearest coin.

"Got you, you little bugger!" Grinning, she grabbed up the lovely thin dimes. "Now all I need is for some woman to answer his phone . . ."

"May I help you?" asked a stern voice behind her.

She had one leg back over the side. Water was streaming onto the carpet as if someone were pouring it through her jeans leg, and the man who was watching her—and wearing a Hyatt name badge—was not amused.

"It's an emergency," she told him, and dashed to the bank of phones.

"What sort of emergency?" he queried, following her, but David's number was already ringing.

"David? I got him!" she cried into the phone. "Hurry! I have him cornered. We're at the Embarcadero."

"Allison?" She'd half-expected him to be asleep, but his voice was clear and he sounded alert. "At the Embarcadero? What are you doing there?"

"I found Cujo! Hurry!" she said, and hung up.

Outside, the derelict had managed not only to guard the dog, but to pet him. He sat on the edge of the cable car monument, patting Cujo's side while the dog slobbered ecstatically and wagged his tail like a metronome.

She came toward him, smiling and grimacing at the same time. "I'm afraid I have some bad news," she said, sitting down next to the man. "I don't seem to have any money with me. But the owner is coming to collect him and I'm sure—"

The man chuckled. "I thought you had an eye for detail," he drawled.

Her lips parted. He was the undercover cop she'd discovered outside Club Hubba Hubba.

She shrugged, feeling sheepish. The man gave her a wink and ambled away, returning to his post on the park bench.

Cujo settled at her feet and began to snooze. She was grateful for his warmth. She was shivering as goose bumps rose on her skin and she tried to wring out her pants. All the damage had occurred from the knees down, so things weren't impossible, but her feet were already turning into blocks of ice.

"So, Cujo, that's the name of that tune," she said, hunching up and stuffing her hands into her pockets.

He grumphed at her and laid his head on the arch of her boot, settling in for a nap. Allison wished she could do the same—she hadn't exactly been sleeping well lately—but she was shivering too hard.

She shivered for what seemed an eternity. Cujo drowsed and dreamed, taking the matter of his rescue with aplomb. It must be nice to have a dog's life, Allison thought as he began to snore.

At last a squeal of breaks announced David's arrival. Allison blinked. He was driving a plain, ordinary pickup truck.

He took his time getting out. Not wanting to startle the dog, she stayed where she was and let David come to them.

"Well, here he is," she announced, a rosy, thrilling warmth immediately supplanting the chill. David's Irish knit sweater molded his large shoulders and jeans molded his small buns. He towered over woman and dog, his eyes not on his long-lost best friend, but on her.

"Aren't you glad to see him?" she went on, gesturing toward the sleeping pup.

"Uh, sure," he replied, then blew his wavy, wonderful hair away from his brow and said, "Allison, I lied to you. I don't own a dog."

"You *what*?" Cujo jerked awake and let out a sharp bark. Allison's blue eyes flashed with fire. "You *don't*?" Then what's this?" She gestured toward the St. Bernard. "And this?" She raised one soaked leg.

"Bad aim?" he asked, trying to make her smile. When she wouldn't, he hung his head in abject remorse. "God, honey, I'm sorry," he murmured, taking her in his arms." I didn't want anything bad to come of this."

"Then why the con job?" she demanded, jerking free. She tore off her fedora and threw it on the ground. "Dammit, David!"

He took her hand in his and brought it to his lips. "You know why, Detective Jones."

A chill of intense pleasure shot through her. She closed her eyes against it and had to force them back open. Her cold hand was enclosed in his, warm and protected. His body shielded hers from the wind; his look softened her indignation.

"I assumed you'd let me help you look for the dog," he explained, picking up her fedora and popping it on her head. "Otherwise I'd never have put you through it. But at least you had to keep calling me with progress reports."

"But . . ."

"Allison, I promised I'd never intrude on you, but now I've got to. I've never asked you for anything, but now I'm going to demand something."

The sky was getting lighter and the light was reflected in her blue eyes. Hope and exhilaration—and yes, fear—

knotted her stomach and pushed their way into her throat.

He looked at the dog. "We can't leave him here," he said. "Maybe it's time for me to have a dog. Even bachelors need love." He looked straight at her. "Let's take him up to the mountains to romp. He needs a break. And so do we."

"I . . ." She couldn't say no. The ache of longing for him welled up inside her and there was no way she could ignore it. It would hurt too much to part from him again.

Although it was going to happen sooner or later, she reminded herself.

She managed a tearful smile. "All right," she whispered. "But I'll have to go home and change first."

"No, let's go now. You can take everything off in the truck—everything that's wet. I have a blanket you can cower under." He wasn't about to risk her changing her mind. If they went to her house, it would be an easy thing for her to opt for some tea, a brief chat, and another brush-off. Dammit, he wouldn't lose her twice!

Be careful, his inner voice warned. Don't crowd her.

"Come on, Allison," he urged, putting her arm around his waist. "Cujo wants you to go, don't you, boy?"

"Woof," Cujo replied.

The three of them walked back to the truck. David put Cujo in back and helped Allison make the ascent into the cab. Before he shut the door, he kissed her tenderly, caressing her earlobe with his thumb. Allison couldn't help responding, drawing air into her chest as his lips seared hers.

"What did you want to ask me?" she whispered when he ended the kiss and prepared to shut the door.

"I already did," he replied. "And you said 'yes.' "

"I didn't realize you meant *way* up in the mountains," she said after they'd driven for two hours. She stretched under the blanket, her bare legs itchy from the wool. "By the time we get there, we'll have to turn back."

"No, we won't. I have a cabin there."

She frowned at him, though her emotions were sky-rocketing. A night alone with him. Even now her body was flashing with desire, heated by the memory of their one night together. David, naked above her, driving her to glorious heights . . .

"Now just a minute!" she protested. "You didn't say anything about spending the night! I don't have any clothes. Who'll take care of my animals?"

"Allison," he interrupted, taking a hand off the wheel and sliding it under the blanket, "hush. It'll be fine. We'll stop at a telephone and you can call the Bionic Woman or Janet to feed those critters of yours."

"But David—"

"Hush." He smiled at her, both hunger and triumph in his eyes.

"How's the chili?" David asked, taking a swallow of beer.

He was sitting at her feet, balancing a plate on his knees. A fire crackled in the stone hearth, throwing dancing shadows on the hardwood floors and open-beamed ceiling. A halo of blue shimmered in his hair as he turned to look at her.

Seated on an overstuffed couch, she was locked in silence. Nerves, she told herself, but it was more than that. It was a waiting, and a yearning, and a knowledge that the only distraction the cabin afforded—food—would soon be gone. There was no radio, no TV, not even a paperback or two to fill the hours of the jet-velvet night. There was nothing but one man and one woman. The electricity that sparked between them grew in intensity as David put down his beer bottle and began to stroke her ankle beneath her stiff jeans, which had dried on a line in front of the fire.

There was the distraction of Cujo. Allison reached down and rubbed his side, snaking her hand through the thick hair.

"Don't," David said. "You'll wake him up."

As if on cue, the dog stirred, raised his head, and moved closer to the fire.

David trailed his fingers from her ankle to her calf. Sharp prickles skittered up Allison's leg, as if it had gone to sleep, traveling higher as David's hand did. They swirled and eddied inside her, currents of sizzling desire that she fought to quell by scooting away from him, crossing her ankles Indian style, and pulling the blanket over her lap.

"I've been missing you," he whispered, pursuing her. "So much. We had some good times, didn't we?"

"Is there any more chili?"

"Didn't we?" He knelt before her, wresting her empty plate from her and putting it on the floor. Cujo ambled over and began to lick it.

"You shouldn't let him do that," Allison said, avoiding David's penetrating gaze. "He'll think he can do it all the time."

"I'll program Gort to zap him. Didn't we?"

Digging beneath the blanket, he laid a hand over her knee. His fingers slid around to the back, fondling it through the worn denim. It was one of her vulnerable placed. Her thigh muscles contracted, creating a rippling effect in her stomach and shoulders, centering in the most sensitive place of all, her feminine core. Rings of sensation fanned out from the soft, wanting place, magic circles that sent out a vibration of love and yearning. His touch gave rise to an even deeper love for him—for everything that made him a man, that made him unique, that made him David.

His hand undulated up the back of her leg. She drew in her breath and he moaned in response, cupping the underside of her bottom.

"Allison, why did you run?" he murmured. "Why, even now, do you hide from me? I don't ask for much . . ." His words trailed off. "You can be whatever you want to be, do whatever you want to do."

When she said nothing, he ran his thumb along the

inner seam of her jeans seductively close to the cleft between her thighs, and sighed.

"If you won't speak, I will," he murmured. "Allison, making love to you was like nothing else in my life. It was . . . unearthly. Your body's so warm and responsive, so sweet and tender." He squeezed her knee. "You were like molten lava surrounding me when I came into you. I've never slept with a woman like you, and I'll be damned if I'll lose something this good without a fight."

Never slept with a woman like her. Not, never loved. Never cherished or wanted, dammit, to intrude a little on her. He didn't care what she did. Hell, he wouldn't care if she were sleeping with somebody else. For all she knew, he was seeing those other women on his list.

"Do you want it?" she asked, tears welling up in her eyes. She lifted his hand and pressed it against herself. "If you want it so much, then take it!"

She burst into tears. At once David gathered her up in his arms, pressing her face into his shoulder as he stroked her temples, her forehead, her lustrous curls.

"Sweetheart, oh, honey, oh, baby," he crooned. "My little love, what's wrong? What's the matter?"

"David, David, I . . ."

She couldn't tell him. He'd leave for sure if he knew she loved him. She remembered his remarks about marriage, how agitated he'd become, how Patricia Courtney had laughed at the mere thought of David King getting married. His friends were even betting against it.

"Shh," he murmured, kissing the crown of her head. "Don't talk."

Perhaps if he hadn't said those words, she would have broken down and confessed. Instead, she nodded mutely and gave herself up to lying in his arms, allowing the sadness to dissipate within the joy of being with him.

She'd try to enjoy the moment, she told herself. She'd savor what they had instead of lamenting what they didn't have.

"I'm sorry," she mumbled, wiping her eyes. "I've had a bad week and I guess I lost control."

"You don't ever have to apologize to me," he said, catching one of her tears with his thumb. His dark eyes glowed with golden warmth, smiling into hers with calm reassurance. "You don't have to do anything you don't want to."

She raised her tear-streaked face. "Including go to bed with you?" she challenged.

He kneaded the triangle between her neck and shoulder with knowing, expert strokes that loosened the knots and forced her to melt against him.

"But you *do* want to go to bed with me." He kissed her, caressing her mouth into yielding compliance. He stroked her upper lip with his, allowing his mouth to part as he breathed against the rosy flesh. He smelled of beer and wood smoke—manly, hearty aromas that filled her as she inhaled deeply.

"Don't you want to?" His lips moved to the corner of her mouth, nipping it ever so lightly, then burning a trail into the soft white skin beneath her jawline. His hands molded her shoulders, massaging away more of her nervousness. "Don't you, Allison?"

Wordlessly she shook her head.

"No?"

"No," she said huskily.

"We'll see about that." His voice rumbled deep in his chest, masculine and throaty.

He stood, then bent down and scooped her into his arms as if she weighed no more than a feather pillow. Flinging the blanket over his shoulders, he began to stride out of the room.

She didn't protest, only widened her eyes questioningly as he took her into the darker recesses of the cabin, past walls covered with Indian blankets and dusty posters advertising hard-to-find car parts.

"There's a loft," he said, turning a corner and starting to climb a flight of roughhewn stairs.

Below, the fire crackled and snapped, billowing

warmth into the nestlike roost at the landing. The jamb was low, nearly brushing David's head as he stopped in the doorway and regarded her.

Over the threshold, he thought, like a bride and groom.

It was pitch-dark inside. David moved gingerly until his foot brushed the corner of a mattress on the floor. He dropped the blanket on top of it, arranging it with one hand while Allison held onto his neck.

"There's a lamp here somewhere," he said, lowering her onto the makeshift bed.

He left her for a moment; she heard him rustling in the darkness. There was a hiss and a small flare, and then she saw his face wreathed in yellow gaslight. He was adjusting the flame on a Coleman lantern set up on an orange crate.

"I'd have thought you'd have a nuclear-powered light," she said, propping herself up on her elbow. Her heart was pounding so hard she was afraid it would bruise her rib cage. Yet she managed to sound casual, as if the crying scene downstairs had never taken place and the kaleidoscope of worries and fears that twisted inside her were nothing more than bits of colored glass.

He sat beside her. "Nope. This is my retreat from the twenty-first century. My friend Bob calls it 'Casa Huckleberry.' " He chuckled. "We had some high old times in this cabin. I hope I can pry his wife off him now and then for a weekend with the guys."

"Marriage *can* be confining," she said blandly, her heart sinking a little.

He shrugged. "Let's not talk about other people. Let's not talk at all."

He lay on top of her, supporting his weight with his elbows. The pale light tamed his uncivilized features as he lifted her hands to his mouth and sucked on her fingers, one by one, never taking his gaze off her. She saw the lines around his eyes and noticed for the first time a hint of gray at his temples—just a few strands, but enough so that they gleamed like silver in the light. She liked noticing it, feeling somehow that she knew a secret of his. She wished she knew more of his secrets, shared more of his life.

"Allison, remember how it was?" he whispered. "Remember how good it felt?"

She nodded, licking her lips as he slid his tongue down the center of her palm and across the beating pulse in her wrist.

"It's going to feel even better," he said, easing her arm above her head.

Her back arched, thrusting her breasts toward him. He lowered his head to the succulent points that strained against the soft down of her sweater, nuzzling them with his face. He caught them between his teeth, pulling her other arm over her head, pinioning her under the weight of his body and the strength of his ardor.

When at last he let go of her arms, she wrapped them around his neck, moving as gracefully as a ballerina, lifting herself off the mattress as he alternately kissed and fondled her breasts. Her curls glistened in the light as she rolled her head from side to side, her breathing growing shallow.

Neither spoke when he pulled her to a sitting position and swept off both sweater and wispy bra. In the warm, scented air she sat before him, her small breasts rosy and full, her eyes filled with love.

"Once we start, there's no turning back," he said cryptically, and she nodded, not understanding what he meant.

He took off her jeans then, and her panties, and parted her legs to admire her. She flushed and tried to close her thighs as she knelt in front of him, but he forbade her.

"You're so beautiful there," he said, fondling her. "Why would you want to hide it from me? You're a tigress," he whispered admiringly. "I've never known a woman so responsive, so filled with fire. Allison, you're incredible."

He rose on his knees, supporting the small of her back as he stroked her. He explored her, discovering again the exquisite way she was made, the petals and the bud, the heady nectar. Covering her with his body, he kissed and licked her breasts, raining adoration on every inch that he could reach.

She heard the quick succession of snaps as he opened his fly. He let go of her back, but she maintained her position, and then he slid inside her, sending a shock wave of sensation through her that almost made her faint.

He cried out. He grabbed her around the waist, thrusting violently, then threw back his head and forced himself to slow down.

"I'm not hurting you, am I, love?" he asked.

Allison couldn't speak. She could barely hear him above the rushing sound in her head. In reply, she pushed against him, seeking, demanding more savage movements. She was on fire, white-hot, lost to thought and awareness of what she was doing. She pushed against him, again and again, feeling no shame or embarrassment at her primitive response, feeling nothing but an implacable desire for more of him.

"Yes," he panted as he obeyed her body's command.

He reared back on his legs and pulled her upward, so that she was rising toward the ceiling. She clung to him, her feet on the mattress, then pushed him backward.

His hands prevented his fall, but he understood what she wanted. Easing himself onto his back, he helped her straddle his hips as he straightened out his legs. Now Allison was on top of him, her hands on his chest, undulating like a harem dancer as she sought to please him.

"Lovely one, lovely one," he chanted over and over. "Allison, my beautiful lady."

Her body was shiny with perspiration. She was steamy and hot and caught in a rhythmic wave that throbbed through her, propelling her toward the summit even as she struggled to contain it. More, more, her body demanded, writhing in David's strong grasp. He filled her being, his essence permeating her like a strong drug that made her senseless with desire.

"Allison, I'm going to come," he whispered, and the words sent her over the brink.

Light shimmered around her, then burst into a thousand stars. She was all the stars and none of them, pulsating with pleasure unimagined even in her wildest fantasies. She was crying and floating and pounding on his chest, and she was no longer herself. She was all women who have ever loved and known the bliss of pleasuring their lovers; all women who have ever lost themselves to utter delight. She was all and nothing; she was everything.

The last sensations contracted within her, sending out charges of electricity that made her dance above him, feeling him within her.

Then David cried her name, clutching her waist, arching so that his back came off the mattress. She felt his release, watched in drained but happy fascination as his body was wracked with the same overwhelming exhilaration as hers.

"Allison!" he cried. "Oh, Allison!"

Then he quieted, his grip on her loosening. His arms fell to his sides and he moaned.

"I'm dead," he announced, exhaling.

She leaned forward, resting her torso on his, wrapping her arms around him. His heart was still thundering.

"I can resurrect you," she said, dotting his face with kisses.

He wove his fingers into her hair. "No pun intended, I suppose."

"Of course not."

He chuckled. His smile faded and he lifted his head to look at her. "Allison, I don't want to lose you," he said, touching her hair, her shoulder, her breast. "I care for you. You mean a lot to me. Life's better when you're around. New again."

He lay his head back and closed his eyes. He'd probably said too much.

"Let's sleep now," he said, urging her head against his chest.

But Allison was too stunned to sleep. She listened to his shallow breathing, tears of confused happiness streaming down her face. He cared for her! He wanted her!

Her face was flushed. David's slumbering body was radiating heat and all at once she had to cool herself down.

She went into the kitchen and turned on the sink faucet, splashing icy water on her face. Calm down, she told herself. Of course he cares for you. All the others did, too.

Just as she turned off the water, two large hands slid around her waist. Crisp male hair brushed her bottom, and a strong, wanting manhood pressed itself against her.

"It's me, Lazarus," David said. "I'm having a miracle. Care to join me?"

Nine

"Hi ho, hi ho, it's through the forest we go!" Allison sang, tapping the rhythm on David's chest. He was loping through the trees, carrying her piggyback, as they resumed their weekend-long game of chase with Cujo.

Allison's clothes were filthy, but she didn't care. She had more brambles in her hair and more mud on her cheeks—and more stickers in her bottom—than she'd had even during her much-frowned-upon tomboy days, but she had never felt better.

"We're on your tail, dog!" David cried, crashing through the underbrush. "Better get a wag on!"

"A wagon?"

"He needs a station wagon," David agreed. "Maybe a Woodie. Remember the surf days, Allison? Baggy bathing trunks and zinc oxide on the old schnozz?"

"Yes, the old glamour days," Allison said. "How I miss my baggy bathing trunks. Just like Dorothy Lamour."

"My nostalgia buff." David laughed. "I don't think the last forty years have occurred in your world. If it were up to you, we'd all be living in black and white."

"My future-fanatic," she countered. "If it were up to *you*, we'd all be robots."

"No way. Your maintenance costs would be too high. I'd have to spend a fortune to keep you well oiled," he said. "Besides," he added with a low chuckle, "I'm right up-to-date on my technology. After all, I already have a precision instrument."

"Oh, brother." She bopped him on the head.

"Well, I do, don't I?" he asked, feigning hurt feelings. He rubbed her breasts with the back of his head, moaning. "Ah, those delectable servomechanisms of yours are charging my batteries, dear one."

"Then stop!" she cried, giggling. "You're charged up enough already!"

Cujo, only feet ahead of them, whirled around and barked at them. Allison bared her teeth and made a menacing gesture, as if to pounce on him. He barked again and zoomed off the path into a dense stand of redwoods.

"Damn, doesn't he ever get tired?" David panted, shifting Allison's weight. "I'm about to collapse!"

"You're out of shape," Allison chided, giving his ear a tweak.

He pretended he was going to drop her, laughing at her squeal as he caught her legs once more.

"Look who's talking! So lazy she even needs a chauffeur to walk!"

"At least it keeps you in business," she retorted saucily.

"That's gratitude for you," David grumbled. "Seriously, though, my love, I'm going to have to put you down or I'm going to get a hernia."

"Oh, Mr. King, you're so romantic. Just like Clark Gable."

He backed up to a rock and lowered her onto it. Then he turned around and took her in his arms. "You're damn right I am, my dear," he said, running his open mouth along the side of her face. "God, Allison, do you think we can make love again?"

Before she could reply, he cupped her breasts and blew gently in her ear. Her body responded instantly, her nipples peaking into erect, tingling buds, ripples jittering between her legs. It was as if she were a candle he had just lit, flaming and melting at once, ready and pliant and shining just for him. He had taught her wonderful secrets during their two days and nights of passion, and her flesh was eager to learn more.

"We'd better not," she murmured reluctantly. "We already agreed we only had time for a short romp."

His brows lifted lazily. "With Cujo," she added, grinning at him and shaking her head.

"There'll be time tonight," he whispered, "once we get home and take care of business. I've probably got a slew of frantic phone calls on my machine. Thank God I forgot my beeper."

"I hope Festina Lente hasn't made a hasty exit to turtle heaven," she said, frowning. "He's not used to the San Francisco climate. He likes the desert. Professor Ptacek's from Albuquerque."

David's hands crept under her sweater and into her bra. He rolled her nipples between his thumbs and forefingers. "Turtle heaven?"

She tried to speak, but chills of pleasure were overcoming her. "Y-yes," she breathed at last. "When I was five, I found my cat Dunbar, 'sleeping' in a ditch. It was my first experience with death. I was inconsolable."

She smiled sadly at the memory, though David's caresses were clouding the sorrow of it. "My Sunday school teacher told me Dunbar couldn't go to heaven because he didn't have a soul. I refused to believe that. I decided that each animal had its own heaven and that Dunbar had gone to cat heaven." She gasped as he pulled the taut peaks. "A child's answer to a difficult concept."

He pulled her against his chest. "Except you still believe it." He pressed his lips to the crown of her hair. "Allison, you are the most tenderhearted hard-boiled gumshoe I've ever met."

"Smile when you say that, G-man," she drawled, thrusting out her lower jaw.

"The littlest Caesar of them all." He feinted a jab. She ducked and tickled his stomach—one of *his* vulnerable places, she'd discovered. He contracted, laughing, grabbing her wrists easily. "Stop that!"

"Never!" she retorted, flailing at him.

"Never say never," he countered, brushing her hair away from her eyes with one hand as he held her wrists with the other. "Never is a long time."

He hugged her against himself, then lowered her to the ground. "Back to earth, tiny one," he said.

"I may be small, but I'm powerful," she retorted, "just like nitroglycerin. Remember, your stomach's within easy reach for me," she said, waving her fingers at him like a hula dancer.

"So's something else," he drawled. "I'm ticklish there, too."

"I don't think 'ticklish' is the right word."

"But it'll do in a pinch," he replied, grinning.

"Oh, you're impossible!" she said, and came for him again.

Cujo bounded up, barking and leaping, eager to join in the fray. Then, all at once, from the very tips of the trees came a breathy, "Oh, damn."

Horrified, Allison looked up, squinting against the morning sun. There, silhouetted against the pink sky, hovered her reformed nephew, once a climber of buildings, now a swinger of redwoods.

"Barry!" she shouted. "Get down from there! Oh, for Pete's sake!"

"Uh, hi, Aunt Al," he said cheerily. "What're you doing up here?"

"I think that's *my* line," she called up to him, jamming her hands on her hips. "Barry, dammit, get down! You could break your neck!" Before I get a crack at it, she added silently.

"Okay, okay. Don't have a spazz attack." He disappeared. Leaves began to rain down on Allison and company as the still morning filled with thrashing noises.

"Do you want me to go up?" David asked, smoothing her sweater over her chest.

She was blushing furiously. What had Barry seen?

She'd been so careful never to do anything with David when he was around! Did he know she'd spent the weekend in David's cabin? Had he seen her standing naked in the moonlight last night, shivering but loving the moment too much to go in?

"No, don't," she said to David. "I don't want to lose both of you."

David's look was odd, his brown eyes soft yet hooded with a secret. "Not to worry," he said, sliding an arm around her waist and kissing her.

Barry's descent was rapid. He appeared at the base of the tree with a coil of nylon around his shoulder and some square pegs and a hammer in his hand.

"Hey, guys," he said. "How's it going?"

"Barry, I could kill you!" Allison cried. "You told me you were on a trip with your class!"

He shuffled his feet. "Well, I was, for a while. But it got boring." He looked past her to David, as if he might get more sympathy there. "See, we never climbed very high. We always passed up the really good mountains."

"The ones that lead to teenager heaven?" David asked, nudging Allison

"When your mother gets home . . ." Allison began, then ran a hand through her hair and sighed. When Maribeth returned, she would do absolutely nothing about Barry's mischief. And from his unconcerned look, Barry knew it.

"Aw, Aunt Allison, I was just having some fun!" he protested.

"We'll talk about it later," she snapped. "Now, come back with us to the cabin. We were just getting ready to go home. How'd you get here, by the way? This is just too much of a coincidence."

Barry trudged behind. "Uh, well, David mentioned the place in one of our talks on the phone. I headed here when I left the climbing party." Cujo fell back from David's side to inspect the new human.

"Whose dog is this?" Barry asked. His voice was high with excitement. "Hey, boy, what's your name?"

Cujo began to lick Barry's face and hands. He ran around him in circles, yipping and panting, twisting this way and that as Barry pretended to grab at him.

"Hey, boy, here, boy!" Barry chanted.

Allison and David traded looks. "A marriage made in heaven?" David asked. "Does Barry have a pet at home?"

"Not that I know of," Allison said. "They certainly are hitting it off, aren't they?"

"Who does he belong to?" Barry asked.

David raised his brows. Allison shrugged.

"He might just be yours," David said. "We'll have to see."

"Far out!" Barry patted Cujo on the back. "Come on, boy!"

They raced past Allison and David, crashing through the underbrush. Soon Cujo's barks echoed in the distance.

"It could be bad for the dog, you know," Allison said. "He might stuff him into a back pack when he attempts Mount Everest."

"It'd have to be a pretty big back pack," David returned. "But Cujo could bring the brandy in his St. Bernard barrel."

"Please, sir, my nephew is a minor."

David glanced up at the towering redwoods. "Who, if he keeps this up, won't live to be a major."

They went back to the cabin and locked up. Barry didn't ask any questions about what they'd been doing there, and Allison didn't offer any explanations. Then they piled into the truck, Barry and the dog in the bed and Allison beside David in the cab.

In spite of her dilemma over Barry, Allison was singing inside as she watched the sun lightening the shadows between the trees and gleaming on the emerald expanses of grass on either side of the road. She was a new woman—one happily, not miserably, in love. She felt light, filled with rainbows and sunshine. In the two short days they'd been together, so much of her fear had slid away. She felt like Olivia de Havilland when Montgomery Clift proposed in *The Heiress*.

It was going to be okay, she told herself as the truck sailed across the bridge. In the distance the skyline of the city rose above the mist. For the first time she dared to hope that this was a man who wouldn't eventually break her heart. They had grown so close during the weekend, sharing each moment with each other in an intimacy she'd never known before.

She reached over and squeezed his hand. He wrapped his fingers around hers and smiled at her, whistling tunelessly.

"Whatcha thinking about, Rosebud?" he asked her.

She leaned her head on his shoulder and ran her other hand along the back of his, feeling the veins. "Oh, just things," she said. "I had such a wonderful weekend, David."

David said nothing, only rubbed his head against hers and continued to drive. Allison felt a flash of worry. Had she said too much? Clung too tightly? But she dismissed it as she listened to David's whistling. He's suave, charming, and handsome, she thought, but he's tone-deaf. He couldn't carry a tune if somebody laid it in his arms. Somehow, that made him all the more endearing.

Then, all too soon, the truck rolled to a stop in front of her house.

"I'd ask you to come in," she said to David, loving the way the sun hit his hair, "but I have to be an aunt for a while."

He touched her cheek. His face grew serious, searching hers, his eyes probing and intent. Their gazes locked and the atmosphere in the truck crackled with tension.

"I want to talk to you about something important," he said finally. "Something I've never contemplated before in my life." He gestured to Barry, who was bounding along the sidewalk with Cujo.

"I know you need to talk to him," he went on, "but I

need you for myself tonight. Can't he spend the night at a friend's?"

She swallowed, not daring to allow herself to admit what she was hoping. That he was going to ask her to . . .

Exhaling, she squared her shoulders and pretended to chomp on a cigar. "Sure, boss. Whatever you say. I'll get ridda da kid."

"I like you this way." He cocked his head and smiled at her. "You were so tight-lipped when I first met you."

"Loose lips sink ships."

"They've sunk me, Allison," he whispered. "I'm drowning. I'll be by at seven to pick you up."

"Let's have dinner over here," she suggested on impulse. "That way we can talk more privately. About whatever you want to talk about," she added, nerves making her chatter.

They regarded each other. Could it be that marriage was—

Oh, God, now that you've uttered the word—even silently—it won't happen, came the thought.

And the thought was in David's head.

And Allison's.

Allison lectured Barry sharply and sent him packing to Eric, one of his mountaineering friends. Tying a bandanna around her curls, she set to work with a feather duster, struggling to make order out of the chaos of her home.

"I'll have to be sure to keep you out of sight," she told the M&M&Ms and the other kittens, late of Rod McKuen's Greatest Hits and now able to toddle about like windup toys.

"He's going to propose, I just know it!" Allison told Hercule as she dusted his beak.

"Stop in the name of the law! Stop in the name of the law!" Hercule replied. Asta, a wirehaired fox terrier who was a new member of the family, chased a dust ball under a chair.

Allison laughed and danced in a little circle. Then she stopped and shook herself. "I could be wrong," she added uncertainly. "It could be something very deflating, like wanting to borrow my fedora."

Ha, her mind retorted. You don't believe that for a minute.

"Well, of course not," she said aloud. "Who'd want to? Besides, he has his own!"

A knock at the door made her heart slam into overdrive. It was only four o'clock. If it was David, she'd kill him.

Well . . .

She opened the door. Hunched in a little ball, convulsing with huge, painful sobs, Janet hurled herself into Allison's arms.

"Hunter's gone!" she wept. "Hunter's gone!"

"Janet, what are you talking about?" Allison asked, stunned. She shut the door with her foot and half-led, half-carried a reeling Janet into her office.

The three white mice popped from beneath the arms of the elephant and nosedived into their box. Hercule breezed in to eavesdrop, landing on his perch. Allison's neon sign flicked on automatically, tinting the tears on Janet's cheeks with lavender.

She cried for a long time, completely out of control, while Allison held her. Stroking her hair, Allison said nothing, only kept her arms around her and rocked her gently.

At last Janet wiped her face with the proffered tissue and honked her nose, apologizing under her breath. Allison waved away her words and handed her another tissue.

"He's fallen in love with somebody in the typing pool," Janet managed to say. "He's moving out, Ally-cat. He doesn't love me anymore!"

"But I thought you two were . . ." Her words trailed off as she realized how insensitive she was being.

Janet's platinum hair shimmered as she ducked her

head. "He kept hinting about big changes. Well, he sure as hell wasn't kidding!"

"Oh, honey, I'm so sorry," Allison crooned, holding Janet again.

"Men," she sobbed. "They tell you they'll always love you, but they lie through their teeth! You were right about them, Allison! I'm never going to get involved again. It's not worth the pain!"

Her lower lip trembled as she looked up at Allison. "Besides, I'll never stop loving Hunter."

"That's how you feel now," Allison said.

Janet shook her head sorrowfully. "No. I'll never forget him."

Allison didn't argue. She understood Janet's need to grieve—after all, hadn't she shed her own share of tears over men?

But those had been tears of hurt and humiliation, she reminded herself. Not those that expressed the deep agony of losing your own true love.

The kind of tears she would shed if David . . .

"Oh, Janet," she blurted out, starting to cry as well, "let's move to Tanganyika! Let's climb Mount Everest with Barry!"

"Wow, he must learn pretty fast if he's up to that already." Janet sniffled.

Allison sighed, wiping her eyes. "I could kill Hunter with my bare hands."

"No, Ally. These things happen. Some people aren't made to stay with one person all their lives, I guess. Hunter had been seeing a lot of other women before we moved in together. I suppose he got . . . wanderlust." She laughed bitterly at her own pun.

They sat in the gathering twilight as the sun drew shadows across the walls. Janet looked small and wan in her chair, slumped into a shell of herself. Every once in a while she heaved a sigh that became a sob, and dusted her nose with the tissue. Allison sat beside her, patting and stroking her arm.

"Do you want a drink?" she asked. "I've got some

Scotch in the bottom drawer." When Janet looked startled, she added, "Just for effect. Marlowe always had a
bottle in his desk."

Janet managed a weak laugh. "I love you, Ally. I'm glad
you were here to lean on."

She'd have to cancel with David, Allison thought.
Whatever he wanted to talk about would have to wait.
Hell, maybe *he* was planning to break it off with *her*.

Allison pulled the bottle out of the drawer, along with
two glasses. When she unscrewed the cap, Janet raised
her hand and shook her head.

"No, Ally. You were cleaning when I came in. That
means big doings here tonight. I'm not going to get
wiped out on booze and ruin your party with David."

Allison poured the liquor, her hand clinking the lip of
the bottle against one of the glasses. She was shaking.

"Don't be dumb. You're my best friend and you're in
the middle of a crisis. David and I can get together some
other time."

"No. I've taken up enough of your time. Besides, I want
to be home while Hunter packs. Who knows?" she went
on with false gaiety. "He might accidentally take my lavender high-top tennies!"

"Oh, Janet," Allison murmured, hugging her tightly.
"Please stay. You can even move in if you want to."

Janet waved her off, smoothing her hair. "No, my
deah," she piped in a British accent. "I must be off. I've
got to run. I'll ring you up tomorrow."

She pirouetted toward the door, then slumped
against the mirror beside it. "Just be careful, Ally," she
croaked, fighting back tears. "Don't you let that David
hurt you."

They looked at each other and embraced once more.
"I'll be careful, Janet," Allison said.

Janet winked at her, a tear trickling down her cheek,
and left. Allison watched her trudge down the street, her
long hair streaming in the breeze.

"I'll be very careful," she said, shutting the door.

*   *   *

He was early. Allison was still feeding her animals when he rang the buzzer. Panicking, she set an opened can of kidneys on a dinner plate and hurried to the door.

"Hi, beautiful," he said, kissing her. He was wearing a charcoal-gray suit with a white shirt and a gray and white tie, and in his arms he carried three dozen roses—a dozen red, a dozen white, and a dozen pink.

"Oh," Allison murmured, overwhelmed. "Oh, David, they're exquisite! I've never seen so many roses!"

"You're exquisite too," he said, standing back to admire her. She was glad she'd put on her black velvet dress—the one she'd worn to that disastrous dinner at his house—and flushed with pleasure as she took the huge bouquet from him and sailed into the kitchen. She began to gather all the vases she had, chattering at him as she did so.

"What a day I had! I really lost my temper with Barry. Then my new dog, Asta, got into a fight with Dirty Harry and Van Helsing. The fur really flew, as they say!" She decided not to tell him about Janet and Hunter. "Uh, how was the rest of your day?"

"Mmm," he replied. He was standing with his back to her in the dining room.

Frowning, she put down the flowers and peeked around the door. "David?" She walked toward him, then burst into a gale of laughter.

He was studying the can of cat food on his plate with a sick grimace. When she laughed, he looked at her dryly and switched plates, wrinkling his nose.

"You have strange taste in hors d'oeuvres, my dear," he said.

"Just very refined," she retorted, picking up the can and carrying it into the kitchen.

After arranging roses in all the vases she could find, there were still piles left over soaking in warm water in the sink. The house was filled with the fragrance of the blossoms, heady and subtle all at once, filled with sweet promise.

But roses wither and die, Allison thought as she

watched David savoring the Beef Wellington she'd cooked. And love—what did love do?

She looked over at him. He was lost in thought. He hadn't spoken much at all since he'd arrived.

He was too busy worrying to indulge in small talk. He could lose her if he didn't do this right, he fretted. If he'd read her wrong, he was in deep trouble.

"Is the beef all right?" she asked, interrupting his anxiety attack.

"It's great," he replied, taking another bite to prove it. "You're a good cook, Allison."

"In my sister's eyes, that's my one redeeming social value," she said flippantly, struggling against the nervousness that was welling up inside her. She didn't think he was acting like a man on the verge of a happy decision. His jaw was set, his lips pulled down into a scowl—definitely a face about to deliver bad news.

David picked up his glass of red wine and held it to the light, then drank slowly. His gaze met hers and he lifted the glass to her lips.

Surprised, she drank, and David's eyes flared with approval. He put down the glass and took her hand, turning it over and tracing the line in her palm. He kissed her scar, the softness of his kiss sending tingles through her body.

"There's dessert," she managed to say, breathing deeply. He was making little circles on her wrist with his tongue, eyes riveted to hers.

"I'll say."

He stood, urging her to do the same. Holding her hand, he began to walk toward the stairs, tender but persistent as he wrapped his arm around her shoulders.

"Is the coast clear?" he asked. "All the cat hairs out of sight?"

"As best as I could manage," she replied, swaying against him. His scent, piney and masculine, mingled with the fragrance of the roses, making her giddy as her body began to anticipate the pleasure that awaited her at the top of the stairs. She leaned her head against his chest as they walked, his thigh rubbing her hip. He was so tall and handsome that he took her breath away.

"Allison, my Allison," he murmured as he led her to the bed, and together they sank down onto it. His hands roamed like swooping eagles over her body. "I love to feel the velvet hugging your breasts," he whispered.

He laid her back against his arm and reached for the vase of roses she'd placed beside a glass lamp on the Egyptian night stand. He threaded the flowers out of the greenery and baby's breath, snapping off the steams, and began to arrange them on the satin pillow, spreading her hair over them.

"You look like the fairy queen resting in her bower," he said huskily. "Like something I've conjured up in my imagination."

He laid his hand over her breast, massaging the swelling firmness. Allison's chest rose and fell and she placed her hand over his. A delicious languor was stealing over her, all rational thoughts sliding away, her nervousness vaporizing. This was David, the man who made love in incredible ways—with fiery passion and with gentle tenderness that made her weep. This was a man who surely was in love.

This was one of the gentle times. He undressed her as carefully as if he were unwrapping a priceless treasure, drawing away her clinging dress to reveal a black lace teddy and a garter belt. The smoky mesh of her seamed stockings silhouetted her thighs and calves as he lifted one leg over his shoulder and kissed her instep.

Then he stood to undress, teasing her the way he had the night of the poker party, revealing the body she now knew so well, and cherished. Then he was towering above her, naked, easing the teddy down, capturing her arms and worshiping her breasts.

He pulled off the delicate garment, leaving her in her garter belt and stockings. Spreading her legs, he paused for a moment, touching her lightly, fondling the secret place that was a secret to him no longer.

"My beauty," he said, then joined his body with hers.

She arched with the delight of it, but he harnessed her passion with his wordless, deliberate thrusts. They looked at each other solemnly as they moved as one, ebbing and flowing like the sea, awash in a silent undercurrent of erotic bliss.

Then Allison was riding the crest. Without crying out, she clung to him, tears running down her cheeks, the moon glowing in her eyes. David joined her, his head thrown back in speechless delight, holding her tightly.

He let his head fall forward as he exhaled. Allison ran her hands through his hair and closed her eyes, lost in deep contentment. David was a consummate lover, a wonderful companion, a fascinating person. She could want nothing more from anyone.

Except commitment, a little voice needled her.

David wiped his forehead and rolled onto his back, covering her hand with his. She felt the absence of his weight like a shock.

He was right, David thought. She did care about him. He didn't think she'd be too upset if he made his proposition. He'd ease her into the idea, and once she saw that it was working out, he'd ask her what he really wanted to—to marry him. But for now, he'd make do with less of a commitment. She'd come around. He knew she would.

He turned on his side and propped his head on his hand. He stroked her face, then splayed his fingers over her collarbones.

"Time to talk," he said, and she nodded, her crystal eyes huge and questioning.

"I've done a lot of thinking about this," he went on, his heart beginning to pound. "I don't suggest this lightly."

What? What? she thought wildly. Say it!

He laid his head over her heart. "You've given me so much," he whispered. "Before I met you, I raced through life trying to grab up every experience I could. I threw a lot away. But you made me stop and look around me. You made me see the colors in the sunset, the curve of the moon against the night. You gave me the smell of flowers and new-mown grass."

She swallowed, lost in his intensity. The roses in her hair were cool and silky against her skin, like the brush of his lips in the first glow of morning.

"For the first time in my life I want to stand still and see everything, touch everything, learn the nuances and subtleties of what's happening to me. Because of you, Allison," he said sincerely.

"Thank you," she whispered, but he laid a finger against her lips.

"And I think we should live together," he said. Before she could react, he held up his hand. "But no heavy commitment. We're free to come and go as we please, as long as we don't hurt each other. I mean, I can have as open a relationship as you want."

Her lips parted in dismay. "Open?"

He shifted on the bed, looking uncomfortable. She wasn't going for it, he thought despairingly. Damn. Time to back off.

"Whatever you want," he assured her. "I don't want to make any demands on you."

"You don't?" she asked in a tiny voice.

"No," he lied.

To his astonishment, she leaped off the bed and backed away, almost as if he had hit her.

"Then the hell with you!" she cried, bursting into tears.

She looked around wildly, then grabbed her dress and covered herself with it. She felt so stupid, so unbelievably ridiculous. *And you thought he was proposing!* she chided herself. *You thought he really loved you!*

"And get the hell out of here!" she added, flying from the room.

"Allison!" David was too stunned to move. By the time he'd jumped off the bed and raced after her, she'd barricaded herself in the downstairs bathroom.

Allison!" He pounded on the door. She was running the faucet. "Dammit, come out of there!"

"Go away! I told you," she said in a choking voice, "that I didn't . . . didn't want to get involved!"

"That's a load of crap!" he shouted, but now he wasn't so sure.

And he was hurt. She was the first woman he'd truly loved, the first. . . . And the mere idea of living with him sent her into a frenzy.

"All right!" he bellowed. "Have it your way. But let me tell you, you are one neurotic lady! When someone cares about you, you act as if . . . Oh, just forget it! I'm sorry I asked!"

He stomped away. Her ear still pressed to the door, Allison continued to let the water run so he wouldn't hear her crying. A tiny, furry head emerged from a towel heaped in the corner and mewed at her. The kitten tottered over and began to nibble her toes as if to comfort her.

Cares? she thought. That's what he thought caring was all about? An open marriage, shack-up style?

Well, why buy the cow when you can get the milk for free? her inner voice asked savagely.

She hit the door with her closed fist. "Just go away, David!" she whispered, sobbing. "Just do it now and get it over."

After a few minutes the sound of the front door slamming told her he'd done just that.

Ten

Three hours later Janet and Allison sat on the floor in Janet's living room, sobbing in unison, passing the last can of diet root beer back and forth like a peace pipe. A weeping Janet had called to ask Allison to come over—Hunter was gone. A weeping Allison had jumped at the chance—so was David.

"It's ironic that we're crying," Allison said, finishing off the can. "I always thought your apartment was such a happy place."

She gestured to the bright clown posters on the walls, the miniature Christmas tree lights outlining the windows, and the vase of parrot-colored pinwheels on top of the TV. Janet's house was an explosion of colors, a celebration of all that was happy-go-lucky. The decor was pure primary color—red and blue and yellow, with splashes of orange and green thrown in. It wasn't the proper setting for a wake at all.

"We're out of diet drinks," she added desultorily. "We'll have to move on to the hard stuff."

Janet shrugged. "Hunter took everything else."

"Swine." Allison sniffled. "Men are beasts. I was right, wasn't I? This always happens to me, doesn't it?"

Janet toyed with the ribbons in her hair for a moment, curling them around her finger and sliding them off. Taking a breath, she scratched her cheek and asked, "What happens?"

Allison blinked at her. "Men always leave me."

"But David didn't leave. You kicked him out."

Allison's eyes flashed, flames dancing in the crystalline blue. "I did not! I . . ." Her voice trailed off. "Well, I had good reason." She frowned.

"Did you?"

Allison leaned back on her elbows and sat Indian style, arranging her legs as she cocked her head at her friend. Janet's face was puffy and red, now it wore a serious look not related to her sorrow.

"I sure as hell did have a good reason!" Allison retorted. "He wanted have his cake and eat it too! He—" She broke off, confused. "Whose side are you on, anyway?"

Janet smiled faintly. "Cupid's. Listen, David probably doesn't know what he wants—except you. He's crazy about you, Ally-cat. Any fool can see that."

"But you yourself warned me against him this afternoon!"

"I was upset. David loves you. He wants to live with you." She hesitated. "Ally, love's so hard to find. Don't throw it away."

Allison's mouth worked. "Now just a minute. You know my past history. The men I've dated . . ."

Janet bit her lower lip and began to work the ribbons again. She didn't look at Allison for a long time. Then she raised her head and said, "I've never said this before, but it's been eating at me for a long time. Those other guys you dated were never right for you. Ed was too straight; Mark was too bizarre. Kevin was always intimidated by your brains. Ally, they left because they were wrong for *you*, not vice versa."

Allison stared at her, her mind racing. That sounded wrong, somehow. Too easy. "You mean, I just pick lousy?"

Janet winked at her. "Usually. But David—now there's a whole new hunk of wax."

"No, it was wrong from the beginning," Allison insisted. "I made a bad choice again. We're not the same at all. I'm old-fashioned, he's Mr. Technology. I'm lower middle class, he's rich. I'm slow, he's fast." She reddened. "Well, usually he's fast."

"You love him," Janet said. "You love him and he loves you. He must love you. Think of what it must have taken for the Bachelor King to ask a woman to live with him!"

"And I want to get married someday and he doesn't." Agitated, Allison stood up and began to pace. "You're wrong, Janet. Wrong about everything. There's just something about me that drives men away."

"Hooey, I say. And how do you know that TDH doesn't want to get married?" she drawled, reaching for a pinwheel and blowing gently on its edge, sending it spinning. "Have you asked him?"

Allison's heart skipped a beat. Janet seemed so sure of what she was saying, so confident. But she wasn't making sense—was she?

"He would've asked me if he'd wanted to," she replied uncertainly. "He's not the marrying kind."

"Oh, huh," Janet snorted, drawing her knees up under her chin. Her long hair fell over her arms like silver rain. "*You* lied to *him*. Why wouldn't *he* lie to *you*?"

Allison's lips parted. "When did I lie?"

"Give me a break. You told him you didn't want to get involved."

"I didn't!"

Janet waved a chastening finger. "You didn't want to get hurt, that's all."

"Exactly. Because men always—"

"Allison, I won't agree with you about that," Janet interrupted. "Yes, you were a lousy picker. You picked guys who didn't fit with you. But then you got lucky. You found somebody who does fit."

"Then why am I going through this?" she cried. "If he's really in love with me, why didn't he tell me so?"

"Same reason as you, dodo. To protect himself." She

shook her head, scrambling to her feet and giving Allison a big hug. "Don't be a sap, kiddo. There are no guarantees in any relationship." She laughed bitterly. "As I can attest. But you and David might just have something that can last, and you're a total idiot if you don't try to hang onto it."

"You're wrong," Allison insisted. "I feel how wrong you are."

But by the time she returned home, she wasn't so sure anymore. Her brain was grinding away at top speed as she put on the teakettle and nuzzled Dirty Harry with her toe. The other animals darted and chattered around her, ecstatic at her return.

"Maybe Janet was right about the other men, the ones who left me," she told Harry. Asta pushed him to one side, panting for a little attention. She laughed and patted his head.

"They weren't appropriate long-term material," she went on. "Maybe my screening devices were working, pushing away men who couldn't handle my personality or my eccentricities—or you guys. Maybe I've been luckier than most women, not building a deep commitment with the wrong person—as Janet did with Hunter."

"Who done it?" Hercule demanded.

"I did," Allison confessed. "I lied to David, over and over. I love him. I want to be involved. Dammit, I want to marry him and have his babies!"

As if on cue, the kittens mewed. Ironside licked their fuzzy bodies and began to transport them back to the record collection. The rooster trotted in her wake.

"So I can either suffer in silence or confess to the crime," she mused, pouring boiling water over the tea bag in her cup. But what if telling him drove him away?

"I'm home free on that score," she murmured wryly. "I've already done that."

"Who done it?" Hercule piped.

"Well, I guess I'm going to," Allison said, grimacing. "Are you guys with me?"

"Rouf!" Asta replied, and the others chorused their agreement.

David looked up from his monthly financial statement and stared bleakly at the fedora sitting on the shelf. He hadn't shaved and his eyes were gritty from lack of sleep. He felt old and tired and utterly defeated.

"But I guess I'm going to win that bet after all," he said wryly. "After all, can't let the guys down, can I?"

He tapped his pencil on the paper and wiped his face with his hands. Should he call or leave her alone? Hound her or try to forget her?

"Or should I kill her?" he muttered. "Wrap my hands around that gorgeous little neck and give it a good—"

He was interrupted by a sharp rap on the door, which opened before he could tell the rapper to go away.

"Yeah?" he barked.

Something barked in response.

It was a tiny golden retriever puppy, in the arms of a short, wiry man wearing a sequined jacket and a black top hat.

"*Bon jour*," the man said in a terrible French accent. "Where do you want ze dog?"

David blinked. "On the desk."

"Very *bon*." He put the tiny puppy on the field of teak. It scrambled toward David, nearly dwarfed by the huge red bow around its neck. Attached to the ribbon was a small white card.

"Who the hell are you?" David asked, staring at the puppy.

"I am Pierre DuBois, of DuBois Limousines," the man informed him haughtily. "I also carry ze finest lines of watches, costume jewelry, and toiletry items, samples of which I have right here in ze briefcase."

He held up a vinyl case and began to open it.

"Here," David said, handing him a twenty without looking at him. "Thanks for the delivery."

"But, *monsieur*, ze watches—"

David cocked his head at the puppy, still not looking

at the man. His throat was closing and his heart was
thundering. Who else would send him a dog? Who else?

"Please, I have ze fine gold jewelry—"

"You'd better work on that accent, friend. Any New
Yorker'll be able to tell right away that you're from
Brooklyn."

The man slumped. "You from da city?" His French
accent had evaporated.

"A suburb. Detroit," David said, dismissing him.
Shrugging, the man put the case under his arm and left.

The puppy stared up at him with huge liquid eyes.
David held out his hand and the creature tottered over
to it, wagging its miniature tail.

Slowly, forcing himself to stay calm, he pulled the card
off the ribbon and opened it.

*Meet me at the foot of the Golden Gate at eight
tonight. No police. No questions. Rosebud.*

He closed his eyes, then bent over and kissed the
puppy on the head. "Thank God," he whispered. "We're
back in business."

In response, the little dog yipped, climbed up on his
arm, and went to the bathroom on his hand-tailored
jacket.

The fog covered the foot of the bridge like a floating
white blanket. It curled and drifted, boiling up to cover
the moon. Tugboats hooted and cars whooshed across
the bridge.

Allison's boots echoed on the pavement as she moved
through the mist. Her heart was pounding, and her
palms were sweating. Her fedora hid her face, but she
knew she was as white as a sheet.

It was eight-fifteen.

He wasn't coming, she thought wretchedly, and
fought back tears. He'd be here already if . . .

She clenched her hands together and paced, kicking
up dust devils of smoky vapor. Tugboats sighed and
moths circled the lights and made little flapping noises
against the bulbs with their wings.

He wasn't coming. He'd be here.

There was a noise, a single footfall. Catching her breath, Allison whirled around.

A tall figure emerged from the shadows. It ambled toward her, shoulders hunched beneath the epaulets of a trench coat, fedora tilted forward at a rakish angle. The streetlamp provided a backlight, silhouetting the figure. The fog rose around it like steam.

"Hey, sweetheart," David said in his best Bogie voice.

She stood transfixed, overcome with happiness and relief.

"Hey, sweetheart yourself," she replied, and ran into his arms.

They rained kisses on each other, Allison straining to reach his chin, but content to pelt his chest and shoulders. David laughed and caught her in his arms, whirling her around, nuzzling her neck, then pulling her against him and burying his face in her hair.

"I was so stupid," he said between kisses. "Allison, I'm sorry."

"*You're* sorry," she retorted as she came up for air. "I was the dodo."

"Listen—"

"Listen—"

They laughed. Allison pressed her hand to his lips, taking the right to speak first.

She squared her shoulders and pushed back her hat, then laid her hand on his chest and said, "I've been lying to you, David. I told you a lot of things . . ." She swallowed. "Living together's for the birds. Let's get married, sweetheart."

When he didn't speak, she began to wilt. Oh, no, she thought. Oh, no, Janet had been wrong. She was wrong. He didn't love her. He didn't want her.

He pushed back his fedora. There were tears in his eyes.

"Oh, darling, thank you," he said. "Thank you for having the courage to do that. God, I love you!" He dropped to one knee before her. "But I was going to ask you the same thing."

A thrill of joy shot through her. She grinned at him and folded her arms in mock hauteur. "Yes, but I asked you first." She broke her pose and caught his face between her hands, kissing his forehead, his temples, his ears and lips. His hair felt like a pelt of mink to her fingertips. She stood back and smiled lovingly at him, dazed, stunned, exhilarated.

"I didn't know what to think," he said. "You didn't want to get involved and—"

"Me?" she interrupted. "What about you, Mr. Swinging Bachelor? What was I supposed to say? 'Here's my heart, stomp on it'?"

He frowned. "Allison, I would never . . . Hey, what are you doing?"

She fished in her pocket and held something up to the light. It was a plain gold wedding band.

"Rosalind Russell would applaud me," she said. "Loretta Young would be appalled. Myrna Loy would smile and offer me a martini." She slipped it on his finger. "It fits."

He chuckled, then rose and held her against him. His heart was racing. He breathed against her hair, then kissed her long and deeply, his tongue seeking and finding hers. It was a kiss that spoke of kisses to come, a lifetime of them.

"Put your hands in my pockets," he murmured.

"David," she said, flushing, "not here."

"My trench coat pockets, you little hot tomato." He ran his tongue down her neck as she obeyed.

In the left one was a small velvet case. Her eyes widened as her fingers wrapped around it.

"David, you didn't," she said, drawing it out.

"Great minds think alike."

Inside was a huge diamond mounted in platinum. On either side of the intricate setting were twinkling star sapphires.

"To match your eyes, my love," David said, kissing her

open palm as he slipped the ring on her finger. Then he molded her hand to his face, nuzzling it with his shoulder. "Joan Fontaine never had better."

"It's beautiful," she whispered. Two tears slid down her cheeks as she looked up at him. "We're going to get married."

"Yes."

"We're going to live together forever."

"Yes."

"We're going to have babies?" she asked uncertainly.

"Yes, yes, yes, yes." He chuckled and touched her lower abdomen, where their children would grow from their love. "That's how many I want—four. Minimum."

Her eyes widened. It was happening, really and truly. Her life was changing. She was going to be his wife, his companion, his lover forever.

Her fingers wrapped around the belt of his coat. "How are we going to manage? Me with my pet detecting and my animals"—she grimaced—"my cats? And that robot kind of made me nervous and—"

He held out his hands. "Hey, lady, *you* asked *me*, remember? Besides, it's elementary, my dear Jones. We'll work it all out because we love each other."

She leaned her head against his chest, hugging him tightly. "Yes, my dear King, we do."

They laced fingers and began to stroll into the fog. David was whistling, but he broke off and looked at her.

"Do you own a rooster?" he asked.

"Yup. Guess his name."

He thought for a minute. "Ralph?"

"No, silly. Alfred Hitchcock."

He groaned, then began to whistle again, grinning at her.

"That's the 'Bridal March,' " he said.

"Could've fooled me."

He put his arm over her shoulder and squeezed her. "I did, Allison. I fooled both of us." He shook his head. "God, I can't believe it. I'm getting married. And I can't

wait!" He turned to her. "Let's elope tonight. We can go
back to your house and . . ."

His voice trailed off, touched by the shining radiance
in her face. She looked like a flower opening to the sun.
"No," he whispered. "I want a real wedding, with you in a
movie-queen gown and a long white veil, and I'll wear a
tux or something, and we'll get Barry to climb the spire
and ring the bell for us."

"And we'll have a tiered cake with doves on top," she
agreed. "All the trimmings."

"Including a bachelor party," Patricia said delightedly
as she gave Allison another hug. "Bob's really looking
forward to this! He's been gloating about taking David to
the Hubba ever since we heard about the engagement.
'Gonna rake that sucker over the coals,' he told me."

Allison laughed merrily. "And it was so nice of you to
arrange this dinner too," she said, watching as the
other men crowded around David and slapped him on
the back. They were still counting up wins and losses in
the bachelor sweepstakes, flashing green and saying
things like, "Hey, Bob, you take credit cards?"

"David is Bob's best friend," Patricia said. "Having a
little get-together to introduce you to everybody was the
least we could do. Mary had a couples' dinner for Bob
and me and I really appreciated it." She gestured to a
small woman with brown hair, who smiled back.

Besides the two of them, eleven other women were
seated in the living room, including Janet and the
Bionic Woman. Captain Curt had come with Emma and
Janet had brought someone new, a violinist who played
the corner across from where she did her street miming.
He was poor and he was a little flighty, but he definitely
had potential.

Allison's mother and father had come for a while, but
Mrs. Jones still had jet lag, though they'd been in town a
week, and wanted to spend the evening "attending to
details." Allison didn't mind. In fact, she was glad to be
able to enjoy the party without having to entertain her

parents. It was time to prop up her feet, have some fun, and meet the wives and girlfriends in David's circle.

"We're going now, my love," Bob called, yanking on David's coat sleeve.

"Don't keep him out too late!" Patricia called back as Bob opened the front door. "Like they did Bob," she added to the other women, who all giggled. "He was so sick!"

"I wasn't *too* sick," Bob said. "See you later!"

David ambled over to Allison and kissed her soundly. The women cheered and applauded.

"Encore!" Mary cried.

David's eyes were shining and eager. "My last night as a free man," he said.

"You'd better believe it, sweetheart," Allison drawled.

Chuckling, he touched her hair, then straightened and looked at the other women. "I hope you won't be too bored without us," he said. "I guess you'll do your bridal shower things, though." He gestured to the pile of pastel packages on the coffee table.

Patricia nodded, folding her hands demurely. "We'll try to live without you boys for a few hours."

"Until tomorrow, then," David murmured to Allison. "Good night, my darling. I'll see you in the morning." His eyes spoke words for her alone: *The morning of our wedding. The morning we give ourselves to each other with such love, such tenderness, that it brings tears of joy to my eyes.*

"Get some sleep," he added, tracing her lips with his finger.

"Surely you jest," she replied, nipping him.

"Aloha, Pat. Don't stay up!" Bob called.

" 'Stay up'?" Stu repeated, horrified. "Knock wood, David. Robert, don't talk like that in front of a bride-groom."

David winked at Allison, a secret wink, and she winked back. Then he joined the rest of the men at the door and they left in a pack, like young, wild wolves.

"Well, shall we do our 'bridal shower thing' like good

little women?" Patricia asked wryly. She turned to Allison. "Tea and crumpets, my dear?"

Allison laughed, knowing the jibes were all in fun. Janet bent on one knee to take her picture as Patricia poured a glass of champagne for her.

They sipped and munched mixed nuts and mints, laughing and chatting, the married women reminiscing about their own bridal showers and wedding days. Allison was effervescent with anticipation. As a young girl she, too, dreamed of her bridal shower and wedding day, but this was better than any dream. She glanced at the spacious room, decorated in ferns and antiques, at the lovely tiered cake, a miniature of her wedding cake, topped with a bride and groom of spun sugar. Everything was more beautiful, more sparkling, than she had ever dared to hope for. The elegant Victorian setting, the lovely, smiling women, the silver and gold decorations that crisscrossed the ceiling, were like things out of a fairy tale. And Allison—without Bacall's golden locks, or Loretta Young's eyes, or Lana Turner's bosom—was going to marry Prince Charming.

They were about to play a party game, finding the things that were wrong in a cartoon wedding portrait, when the doorbell rang.

"Oh, that must be the crumpets now," Patricia said, rising.

"I've always thought the men had all the fun at those bachelor parties," Janet murmured to Allison. "I mean, this is neat, but . . ."

"Hey, ladies! Where's the bride?" a deep male voice demanded.

All heads turned toward the door. A magnificent blond man was standing there, wearing a tight-fitting satin shirt and black pants, holding a dozen balloons and carrying a tape recorder. "Where's the lady of the evening?"

"Here! Here!" Mary called, pointing at Allison. Flushing, Allison buried her face in her hands.

"All right!" the man cried. "Hey, Allison Jones, I'm here to thrill your bones! I'm tall and sweet, your wedding eve treat, I'm Gorgeous Greg from Stripogram on Turk Street!"

He strutted over to her, handed her the balloons, and bussed her on the lips. Then he set down the tape recorder and struck a pose, feet wide apart, hands over his head.

A disco beat pulsated. Gorgeous ground his pelvis in a wide circle right in front of her face. Allison's mouth dropped open and she looked at Patricia. Patricia grinned slyly and mouthed, "Just a bridal shower thing."

A frenetic version of the "Bridal March" caught up with the beat, and Greg yanked off his shirt, revealing a broad muscleman's chest and arms.

The women burst into squeals of shocked laughter. Greg twirled in a circle, flexing his muscles. "Hey, Allison King, hope love is your thing!" he chanted.

"I take it all back," Janet whispered to Allison, laughing. "I hope David has as much fun as you do."

Now Greg was threatening to whip off his pants.

Allison covered her burning cheeks with her hands. "Good Lord, Janet, I hope David doesn't!"

"Don't worry, ladies!" Greg boomed. "It's all done with Velcro!"

And off came the trousers.

From her chair in front of the dressing table mirror, Allison could see David sitting on the bed and pulling off his pants. She watched, fascinated, as his body was revealed to her, the light from the fireplace flickering on his muscular thighs.

The twelfth night of their honeymoon and she was still dizzy with joy. England had been another dream, even including a visit to the Morgan plant. And today, in Italy, they'd had a tour of the Ferrari plant. David's enthusiasm for luxurious cars was infectious, and she found his intense excitement endearing. They'd stay a few more days here in the honeymoon suite of a refurbished Italian farmhouse, then it was north to Stuttgart, home of the Porsche and the Mercedes-Benz. They were staying in a castle there, he'd told her.

She set the brush down and walked toward her husband. A white negligee floated around her, drifting open to reveal a clinging satin gown that silhouetted the curves of her body, the rising peaks of her nipples. On her feet she wore satin sandals decorated with tufts of ostrich feathers across the toes.

David looked up from pulling off his underwear and reached for her, urging her onto his lap. He regarded her, love glowing on his face, his large hands wrapping around her small body.

"You look so beautiful," he said, "so glamorous."

"As glamorous as Rita Hayworth?" she demanded, striking a pose.

He drew the negligee away and kissed her bare shoulder. "No. More glamorous. She's a hag compared to you." He reached over and poured her a glass of ruby wine, testing it before he held it to her lips.

"Are you having fun, love?" he asked. "You don't mind touring the car factories? Am I dragging you across Europe too fast?"

"No complaints," she replied, settling her arms around his neck. Beneath her bottom, she felt his manhood begin to respond to her. There was heat and strength there, and she moved her hips to caress him with her satin gown.

"Are *you* having fun?" she asked him, nuzzling his chin.

"Yeah," he murmured, taking the wine away from her. He slid her off his lap and laid her on the bed, then rolled beside her and filled his hands with her breasts. "I sure am." He drew his tongue across the valley of her cleavage, dotting the gently swelling with kisses as he pressed his hands around her hips.

"I know of a way to have a lot more fun," Allison whispered, undulating with each move he made.

David's lids grew heavy, his smile languid. "Mmm? How?"

Oh, I love him, how I love him, she thought, her heart singing. She reached for him, drawing him to her. "I'll show you, my husband," she said breathlessly.

She pushed him onto his back and bent over him, stroking and fondling his shoulders and arms, teasing his tiny nipples into awakening, taut points. He groaned, and she pulled her gown up to her waist and straddled his hips.

"Allison, oh, Allison," he said hoarsely, gasping as she took him into herself. "Thank God I found you!"

"Finders keepers, my love," she said, beaming with happiness. "I'm yours forever." She laid her head on his chest, listening to his wild heartbeat. "And you're mine," she added, tears of emotion sliding onto the dark hair.

They moved in a crescendo of love and desire. "Yes," David told her, clinging to her in the Italian moonlight. "Yes!"

THE EDITOR'S CORNER

Last month I told you about the long novels coming from LOVESWEPT authors in the Bantam Books' general list. And now this month you get a special treat: an excerpt from Sandra Brown's riveting historical romance, **SUNSET EMBRACE**. It's right in the back of this book and I'm sure the brief glimpse into the lives of Lydia and Ross will intrigue you so much that you'll want to ask your bookseller to hold a copy of **SUNSET EMBRACE** for you. It's due on the racks early next month.

Sandra really packs a double whammy for romance readers next month because you can also look forward to a LOVESWEPT from her! And "double whammy" is not only apt for the long historical plus short contemporary publication, but as a description of her LOVESWEPT #79. In **THURSDAY'S CHILD** heroine Allison is a twin. And she is persuaded to "pull a switch" by her sister Ann who couldn't be more different from Allison if she'd been born to other parents. And then along comes Spencer Raft—one of those extraordinarily dashing and sensual men that Sandra dreams up—and scientist Allison is the beneficiary of some very special "experimental" help from Spencer. **THURSDAY'S CHILD** is so humorous and has such wonderful love scenes that you definitely will *not* want to miss it!

With only two romances published (**BREAKING ALL THE RULES,** LOVESWEPT #61 and **CHARADE,** LOVESWEPT #74), Joan Elliott Pickart has certainly found her place in readers' hearts. Joan and all of us

(continued)

here are very grateful for your letters praising those books. Well, here's cause for rejoicing about her romances again: **THE FINISHING TOUCH,** LOVESWEPT #80. Paige Cunningham is one of the most heart-warming of heroines. I was routing for her from first word until last as she and Kellen Davis fell in love and confronted their problems. Paige is an interior decorator and Kellen is an actor. She is working on his new home and there are some truly comic scenes as Kellen traipses along to help her shop for furnishings. And there is a love scene of such compassion and tenderness between them that I am positive you will never forget **THE FINISHING TOUCH.**

I found Joan Bramsch's offering for next month—**THE LIGHT SIDE,** LOVESWEPT #81—a marvelous romance . . . spritely, downright funny and terribly touching. Savvy Alexander entertains at children's parties dressed as a clown. Balloons are her "signature," and when she meets hero Sky Brady she's in an elevator (stuck!) that's crammed with balloons. Sky comes to the rescue, but very soon decides he needs rescuing—emotionally—from one dynamite little lady clown. But there are major obstacles to overcome before these two wonderful folks can find true, committed love. **THE LIGHT SIDE** has its serious side too and will appeal to all your emotions.

Last—but never, never least—Iris Johansen is back! Iris interrupted work on her second long novel for Bantam to write two LOVESWEPTS. First, you'll delight in **WHITE SATIN,** LOVESWEPT #82, in which Iris portrays the trials and tribulations of Dany Alexander. Dany is reaching to win the gold in Olympic ice skating competition while trying desperately to achieve happiness with her mentor Anthony Malik. This is a love story in typical "Iris Johansen tradition"—glowingly emotional, fast-paced, and as deliciously sensual as that title, **WHITE SATIN.** Now, you know our lovably tricky Iris, so you'd better read carefully if you want to discover which of the secondary characters in **WHITE SATIN** will be the hero of her LOVESWEPT #86, coming month after next, **BLUE VELVET.**

May your New Year be filled with all the best things in life—the company of good friends and family, peace and prosperity, and, of course, love.

Warm wishes for a wonderful 1985 from all of us at LOVESWEPT,

Carolyn Nichols

Carolyn Nichols
  Editor
LOVESWEPT
Bantam Books, Inc.
666 Fifth Avenue
New York, NY 10103

Read this special preview of

Sunset Embrace

by Sandra Brown

Coming from Bantam Books this January

They were two untamed outcasts on a Texas-bound wagon train, two passionate travelers, united by need, threatened by pasts they could not outrun. . . .

Lydia Russell—voluptuous and russet-haired, fleeing from a secret shame, vowing that never again would a man, any man, overpower her. . . .

Ross Coleman—dark, brooding, and iron-willed, with the shadow of a lawless past in his piercing eyes, sworn to resist the temptation of his wanton longings. . . .

Fate threw them together on the same wild road, where they fought the breathtaking desire blazing between them, while the shadows of their enemies grew longer. As the wagon train rolled west, the danger of them drew ever closer, until a showdown with their pursuers was inevitable. Before it was over, Lydia and Ross would face death . . . the truth about each other . . . and the astonishing strength of their love. . . .

She liked the way his hair fell over his forehead. His head was bent over as he cleaned his guns. The rifle, already oiled and gleaming, was propped against the side of the wagon. Now he was working on a pistol. Lydia knew nothing of guns, but this particular one frightened her. Its steel barrel was long and slender, cold and lethal. Ross brought it up near his face and peered down the barrel, blowing on it gently. Then he concentrated on rubbing it again with a soft cloth.

Their first day of marriage had passed uneventfully. The weather was still gloomy, but it wasn't raining as steadily or as hard as it had been. Nevertheless, it was damp and cool and Lydia had spent most of the day in the wagon. Ross had gotten up early, while it was still dark, and had shuffled through trunks and boxes. He seemed intent on the task, and she had pretended to sleep, not daring to ask what he was doing. When she did get up and began to move about the wagon she noticed that everything that had belonged to Victoria was gone. She didn't know what Ross had done with Victoria's things, but there was nothing of hers left in the wagon.

Lydia watched him now as he unconsciously pushed back his hair with raking fingers. His hair was always clean and glossy, even when his hat had mashed it down. It was getting long over his neck and ears. Lydia thought the black strands might feel very good against her fingers if she ever had occasion to touch them, which she couldn't imagine having the nerve to do even if he would allow it. She doubted he would. He treated her politely, but never commenced a conversation, and certainly never touched her.

"Tell me about your place in Texas," she said softly, bringing his green eyes away from the pistol to meet hers in the glow of the single lantern. She was holding the baby, rocking him gently, although he had finished nursing for the night and was already sleeping. They were killing the minutes until it was time to go to bed.

"I don't know much about it yet," he said, turning his attention back to his project. He briefly told her the same story about John Sachs that he had told Bubba. "He sent for the deed and, when it came back in the mail, there was a surveyor's description attached to it."

His enthusiasm for the property overrode his restraint and the words poured out. "It sounds beautiful. Rolling pastureland. Plenty of water. There's a branch of the Sabine River that flows through a part of it. The report said it has two wooded areas with oak, elm, pecan, cottonwoods near the river, pine, dogwood—"

"I love dogwood trees in the springtime when they bloom," Lydia chimed in excitedly.

Ross found himself smiling with her, until he realized he was doing it and quickly ducked his head again. "First thing I'll have to do is build a corral for the horses and a lean-to for us." The word had fallen naturally from his lips. Us. He glanced at her furtively, but she was stroking Lee's head and watched the dark baby hair fall back into its swirls after it was disturbed. Lee's head was pillowed on her breasts. For an instant Ross thought of his own head there, her touching his hair that way with that loving expression on her face.

He shifted uncomfortably on his stool. "Then, before winter, I'll have to build a cabin. It won't be fancy," he said with more force than necessary, like he was warning her not to expect anything special from him.

She looked at him with unspoken reproach. "It'll be fine, whatever it is."

He rubbed the gun barrel more aggressively. "Next spring I hope all the mares foal. That'll be my start. And who knows, maybe I can sell timber off the land to make some extra money, or put Lucky out to stud."

"I'm sure you'll make a success of it."

He wished she wouldn't be so damned optimistic. It was contagious. He could feel his heart accelerating over the unlimited prospects of a place of his own with heavy woods and fertile soil, and a prize string of horses. And he wouldn't have to be looking over his shoulder all the time either. He had never been in Texas. There wouldn't be as much threat of someone recognizing him.

Lost in his memories, he snapped the barrel back into place, spun the loaded six-bullet chamber, and twirled the pistol on his index finger with uncanny talent before taking aim on an imaginary target.

Lydia stared at him with fascination. When it occurred to Ross what he had done out of reflex, he jerked his head around to see if she had noticed. Her dark amber eyes were wide with incredulity. He shoved the pistol into its holster as if to deny that it existed.

She licked her lips nervously. "How . . . how far is your land from Jefferson?"

"About a day's ride by wagon. Half a day on horseback. As near as I can figure it on the map."

"What will we do when we get to Jefferson?"

She had listened to the others in the train enough to know that Jefferson was the second largest city in Texas. It was an inland port in the northeastern corner of the state that was connected to the Red River via Cypress Creek and Caddo Lake. The Red flowed into the Mississippi in Louisiana. Jefferson was a commercial center with paddle-wheelers bringing supplies from the east and New Orleans in exchange for taking cotton down to the markets in that city. For settlers moving into the state, it was a stopping-off place where they purchased wagons and household goods before continuing their trek westward.

"We won't have any trouble selling the wagon. I hear there's a waiting list for them. Folks are camped for miles around just waiting for more wagons to be built. I'll buy a flatbed before we continue on."

Lydia had been listening, but her mind was elsewhere. "Would you like me to trim your hair?"

"What?" His head came up like a spring mechanism was operating it.

Lydia swallowed her caution. "Your hair. It keeps falling over your eyes. Would you like me to cut it for you?"

He didn't think that was a good idea. Damn. He *knew* that wasn't a good idea. Still, he couldn't leave the idea alone. "You've got your hands full," he mumbled, nodding toward Lee.

She laughed. "I'm spoiling him rotten. I should

have put him in his bed long ago." She turned to do just that, tucking the baby in a light blanket to keep the damp air off him.

She had on one of the shirtwaists and skirts he had financed the day before. He wasn't going to let it be said that Ross Coleman wouldn't take care of his wife, any more than he was going to let it be said that he was sleeping outside his own wagon when he had a new wife sleeping inside. It was hell on him and he didn't know how he was going to survive many more nights like the sleepless one he had spent last night. But his pride had to be served. After a suitable time when suspicions would no longer be aroused, he would start sleeping outside. Many of the men did, giving up the wagons to their wives and children.

She liked those new clothes. She had folded and refolded them about ten times throughout the day. Ross couldn't decide if she was a woman accustomed to having fine clothes who had fallen on bad times, or a woman who had never possessed any clothes so fine. When it came right down to it, he didn't know anything about her. But then, she didn't know about him either, nor did anyone else.

All he knew of her was that a man had touched her, kissed her, known her intimately. And the more Ross thought about that, the more it drove him crazy. Who was the man and where was he now? Every time Ross looked at her, he could imagine that man lying on her, kissing her mouth, her breasts, burying his hands in her hair, fitting his body deep into hers. What disturbed him most was that the image had begun to wear his face.

"Do you have any scissors?"

Ross nodded, knowing he was jumping from the frying pan into the fire and condemning himself to another night of sleepless misery. He wanted badly to hate her. He also wanted badly to bed her.

He resumed his seat on the stool after he had given her the scissors. She draped a towel around his neck and told him to hold it together with one hand. Then she stood away from him, tilting her head first to one side then the other as she studied him.

When she lifted the first lock of his hair, he caught her wrist with his free hand. "You aren't going to butcher me, are you? Do you know what you're doing?"

"Sure," she said, teasing laughter shining like a sunbeam in her eyes. "Who do you think cuts *my* hair?" His face drained of color and took on a sickly expression. She burst out laughing. "Scared you, didn't I?" She shook off his hand and made the first snip with the scissors. "I don't think you'll be too mutilated." She stepped behind him to work on the back side first.

His hair felt as good coiling over her fingers as she had thought it would. It was course and thick, yet silky. She played with it more than she actually cut, hoping to prolong the pleasure. They chatted inconsequentially about Lee, about the various members of the train, and laughed over Luke Langston's latest mischievous antic.

The dark strands fell to his shoulders and then drifted to the floor of the wagon as she deftly maneuvered the scissors around his head. It was an effort to keep his voice steady when her breasts pressed into his back as she leaned forward or glanced his arm as she moved from one spot to another. Once a clump of hair fell onto his ear. Lydia bent at the waist and blew on it gently. Ross's arm shot up and all but knocked her to the floor.

"What are you doing?" Her warm breath on his skin had sent shafts of desire firing through him like cannonballs. His hand all but made a garrote out of the towel around his neck. The other hand balled into a tight fist where it rested on the top of his thigh.

She was stunned. "I . . . I was . . . what? What did I do?"

"Nothing," he growled. "Just hurry the hell up and get done with this."

Her spirits sank. They had been having such an easy time. She had acutally begun to hope that he might come to like her. She moved around to his front, hoping to rectify whatever she had done to startle him so, but he had become even more still and tense.

Ross had decided that if she were to trim his hair, it was necessary for her fingers to be sliding through it. He had even decided that it was necessary for her to lay her hand along his cheek to turn his head. He had decided that this was going to feel good no matter how much he didn't want it to and that he might just as well sit back and enjoy her attention.

But when he had felt her breath, heavy and warm and fragrant, whispering around his ear, it had all the impact of a strike of lightning. The bolt went straight from his head to his loins and ignited them.

If that weren't bad enough, now she was standing in front of him between his knees—it had been only natural to open them so she could move closer and not have to reach so far. Her breasts were directly in his line of vision and looked as tempting as ripe peaches waiting to be picked. God, but didn't she know what she was doing? Couldn't she tell by the fine sheen of sweat on his face that she was driving him slowly crazy. Each time she moved, he was tantalized by her scent, by the supple grace of her limbs, by the rustling of the clothes against her body which hinted at mysteries worth discovering.

"I'm almost done," she said when he shifted restlessly on the stool. Her knees had come dangerously close to his vulnerable crotch.

Oh, God, no! She leaned down closer to trim the hair on the crown of his head. Raising her arms higher, her breasts were lifted as well. If he inclined forward a fraction of an inch, he would nuzzle her with his nose and chin and mouth, bury his face in the lushness and breathe her, imbibe her. His lips, with searching lovebites, would find her nipple.

He hated himself. He plowed through his memory, trying to recall a time when Victoria had been such a temptation to him, or a time when he had felt free to put his hands over her breasts for the sheer pleasure of holding them. He couldn't. Had there ever been such a time?

No. Victoria hadn't been the kind of woman who deliberately lured a man, reducing him to an animal. Every time Ross made love to Victoria it had been with reverence and an attitude of worship. He had entered her body as one walks into a church, a little ashamed for what he was, apologetic because he wasn't worthy, a supplicant for mercy, contrite that such a temple was defiled by his presence.

There was nothing spiritual in what he was feeling now. He was consumed by undiluted carnality. Lydia was a woman who inspired that in a man, who had probably inspired it as a profession, despite her denials. She was trying to work the tricks of her trade on him by looking and acting as innocent as a virgin bride.

Well, by God, it wasn't going to work!

"Your moustache needs trimming too."

"What?" he asked stupidly, by now totally disoriented. He saw nothing but the feminine form before him, heard nothing but the pounding of his own pulse.

"Your moustache. Be very still." Bending to the task, she carefully clipped away a few longish hairs in his moustache, working her mouth in the way she wanted his to go.

Had he been looking at her comical, mobile mouth, it might have made him laugh. Instead he had lowered his eyes to trace the arch of her throat. The skin of it looked creamy at the base before it melded into the more velvety texture of her chest that disappeared into the top of her shirtwaist. Did she smell more like honeysuckle or magnolia blossoms?

Every sensory receptor in his body went off like a fire bell when she lightly touched his moustache, brushing his lips free of the clipped hairs with her fingertips. First to one side, then the other, her finger glided over his mouth. The choice was his. He could either stop her, or he could explode.

He pushed her hands away and said gruffly, "That's enough."

"But there's one—"

"Dammit, I said that's enough," he shouted, whipping the towel from around his neck and flinging it to the floor as he came off the stool. "Clean this mess up."

Lydia was at first taken off guard by his rudeness and his curt order, but anger soon overcame astonishment. She grabbed his hand and slapped the scissors into his palm with a resounding whack. "You clean it up. It's your hair. And haven't you ever heard the words 'thank you' before?"

With that she spun away from him and, after having taken off her skirt and shirtwaist and carefully folding them, crawled into her pallet, giving him her back as she pulled the covers over her shoulders.

He stood watching her in speechless fury before turning away to find the broom.